Legends of
Longdendale

Thomas C. Middleton

Legends of Longdendale

The present edition is a reproduction of previous publication of this classic work. Minor typographical errors may have been corrected without note; however, for an authentic reading experience the spelling, punctuation, and capitalization have been retained from the original text.

ISBN: 978-1-64439-635-3

To

Frederick Higham,

of

Abbotsford, Godley Green, Hyde,

in memory of

Happy Hours spent together in Literary Association,

and for the sake of

A Friendship which ripens as the Years pass,

This Book of

Legends of that Wild Land we both Love,

is Dedicated

by

The Author

Contents

Preface

HITHERTO, the Legends of Longdendale—although popular with the country people of the extreme north-east corner of Cheshire—have been scattered, and, to some extent, fragmentary. They are here re-told in what, I hope, is a more permanent and complete form. As far as possible I have carefully followed the original versions; but in one or two instances, it has been necessary to draw upon imagination. I have, therefore, introduced several characters and incidents for the purpose of giving local connection and completeness to those stories which were lacking in detail or were vague in location. The legends are here printed in chronological order. They were first published in the columns of the "Cheshire Post" during the winter of 1905-6; and it is to the kind encouragement and assistance of Mr. Frederick Higham, the proprietor and editor of that journal, that they owe their appearance in book form.

If further explanation as to the publication of these stories be considered necessary, I would refer the reader to the Preface to the first series of "The Traditions of Lancashire." In it Mr. Roby quotes the following passage from a German writer:—"All genuine, popular tales, arranged with local and national reference, cannot fail to throw light upon contemporary events in history, upon the progressive cultivation of society, and upon the prevailing modes of thinking in every age. Though not consisting of a recital of bare facts, they are in most instances founded upon fact, and in so far connected with history, which occasionally, indeed, borrows from, and often reflects light upon, these familiar annals, these more private and interesting casualties of human life. It is thus that popular tradition connected with all that is most interesting in human history and human action upon a national scale, ... invariably possesses so deep a hold upon the affections, and offers so many instructive hints to the man of the world, to the statesman, the citizen, and the peasant."

I may add to the above the fact that these wild and improbable tales have a fascination for me, and that I firmly believe it to be the duty of the people of the present to preserve from oblivion the traditions of the past. In the case of the County of Lancaster, this preservation has been admirably carried out by the late John Roby; and it is with the desire to perform a similar service for the County of Cheshire—or at least one corner of it,—that I have ventured to write the stories which appear in this volume.

THOMAS MIDDLETON

Manchester Road,
Hyde
1906

I

The Legend of Coombs Rocks

FOR some time after the invasion of Britain by Julius Cæsar (55 B.C.) no proper steps were taken by the Romans to reduce to submission the northern portion of the island. The civil war in Rome, which resulted in the establishment of a monarchy under Augustus, prevented the Romans from making further attempts upon Britain, for Augustus was unwilling to endanger the empire by extending its limits. At length, however, the Emperor Claudius, remembering the island, sent over an army which carried the Roman line beyond the Thames. Later in the same reign the Romans subdued an insurrection among the Brigantines—a nation which inhabited Lancashire, Yorkshire and the other Northern counties. The kingdom of the Brigantines extended to Longdendale, where it was bounded by the territory of the Cornavii, another ancient British tribe who were masters of Cheshire and several other counties to the south of the Brigantine line. These warlike tribes again rose in opposition to the Romans, but were finally subdued by Julius Agricola, who, coming to Britain about the year 79 A.D., took possession of Cheshire, and occupied the county with his own legion. He is supposed to have either led or sent a strong force of soldiers to overcome the inhabitants of Longdendale, and one outcome of this expedition was the series of incidents narrated in the following legend.

It would be about the year 80 A.D. when the Romans advanced up the north-east Horn of Cheshire to attack the people of Longdendale. Agricola heralded his coming by a summons to surrender, which was met by a defiant refusal from the haughty Britons. Proud of their country and her great traditions, the local Britons determined to fight for their freedom to the last, preferring death in battle to slavery beneath the yoke of Rome.

"Tell thy proud chief that the sons of Britain are warriors and free men. Free men will they live, and free men die. Never will they

1

submit their necks to the yoke of the Eagle. Rather will they perish on the spears of the legionaires."

Thus spoke Edas the son of Atli, the brave hill warrior, who was chief of the Britons in Longdendale. The Roman heard, and, proud and haughty though he was, could not help admiring the heroic audacity of the white, half naked savage who stood before him. Edas, son of Atli, was a finely built man, six feet and more in height, broad of chest and stout of limb, and standing thus, with no garment save a covering of wolf-skin about his loins, the beautiful proportions of his frame stood out with the clearness of a statue. His long hair hung loose about his shoulders, shining golden in the sunlight, and truly was it said of him that no hero of the old time was more glorious to look upon.

For a moment the Roman paused. Then at length he spake.

"Why battle with the legions? Why fight against fate? Why not live as free men? To be a citizen of Rome is to be a free man indeed—a citizen of an empire which rules the world. Welcome the Eagles and live. But resist the legions, and—what then?"

"Then," replied Edas, "we shall at least preserve our honour; we shall at least remain free as our fathers were; we shall have the chance to emulate the deeds, and die deaths as glorious as those of the heroes of whom the bards sing, and we shall not live to see our wives and daughters dishonoured by the ruthless soldiers of Rome."

He looked the Roman full in the face, and the emissary of Agricola flushed with anger at the implication contained in the chief's concluding words.

"Is that all?" he asked. "Is that thy message to Agricola? Not peace but war?"

"War," answered the chief fiercely. "War to the death against the Romans."

"So be it. The legions will surely come. Farewell."

A short time only elapsed after the dispatch of this defiant declaration ere the British outposts brought news of the Roman advance. Perfect master of the art of war, Agricola left nothing to the last moment, and the same day which brought the message from the Britons, saw the Roman army in motion. The troops

2

marched along the course of the Mersey, and halted for a space at Stockport, where they afterwards built a strong station. Then they moved on, still following the stream, and passed up the banks of the river Etherow, until the great basin of the Coombs Valley lay before them.

Meanwhile the Britons had vigorously prepared themselves for the great struggle. Over the heathery wastes of the hills—into what are now the counties of Lancashire, Yorkshire, and Derbyshire—through the thick forests where the wolves, bears, and other wild beasts of prey lurked—went the war message of Edas the chief, rallying the warriors to battle. For once the tribal jealousies were forgotten, feuds vanished in face of the common danger, and Brigantines joined with Cornavii to offer a united front to the common enemy. For days succeeding the arrival of the Roman herald there was a great massing of warriors, fleet-footed graceful men from the Cheshire plains, big wild men from the mountains which lie to the north and east of Longdendale. Day and night the forest altars and the stone circles of the Druids, which stood amid the heather on the summit of the Coombs, were constantly the scenes of sacrifices and other savage rites of Druid worship. Young men and maidens were slain by the golden knife of the Arch Druid, and their spirits passed, with the strains of weird singing, to intercede with God for the cause of Britain. All day the bards sang the songs of old, and at night the ghosts of buried heroes sailed past on the wings of the wind. Thus were the hearts of the British warriors strengthened for the battle which was to come.

Night fell, and the forests of Longdendale were full of the white, fierce warriors, who moved silently yet swiftly in the direction of the Coombs. It was the last night of peace; on the morrow the songs of war would arise, and brave men would die. Also, it was the night of sacrifices, and the Druid altar—that strange group of stones now known as the Robin Hood's Picking Rods— would witness the supreme sacrifice—the offering to the Gods of that which was most dear to the hearts of the Britons. That day, just before the setting of the sun, Arwary, the fleet-footed, had bounded into the camp with the lightness of the deer, bringing tidings of the Roman advance. The legions would attack on the morrow, and so

3

that night must be a night of sacrifice—the greatest sacrifice of all. Caledon, the ancient Druid, had summoned the Druid priests to the sacred groves of oak, and the warriors were bidden to gather about the altar shortly before the rising of the moon.

In the wood, near the dwelling of Edas, stood the chief. By his side was a maid—Nesta the fair—the beloved of Edas, son of Atli. Soon, if the gods willed, she would become his bride. Meanwhile she was the fairest maid in all Britain, and even the voluptuous Romans sang her praises about the camp fires at night.

Edas, son of Atli, spoke of love, and Nesta the fair drew close to his breast. Her arms were about his neck, and the lovers kissed. Edas, son of Atli, and Nesta the Fair, were happy.

Presently a voice was heard, and the maiden started. It was the voice of Caledon, ancient Druid and he called for Nesta the Fair.

"The gods have need of thee," he cried. "They have sent to me their message, and they ask as a sacrifice the beloved of Edas— the bride of the chief."

The voice of the Druid was stern and terrible. Edas the chief stood like one bereft of reason. Only Nesta the Fair remained calm.

"It is the will of the All-Giver," she said, and sighed. "Yet—I had dreamed of happiness and love."

Again the voice of Caledon cried—

"What greater happiness can a maiden have than to be the chosen of the gods?"

But Edas flung his arms about the maid.

"She is too young, too fair to die," said he, his voice breaking with agony. "Druid, it shall not be."

For a moment the priest stood silent. Then the words fell from his lips in an angry torrent.

"Art thou a coward, Edas, son of Atli? Must the daughters of the poor be offered for sacrifices, and shall the mighty ones of the earth escape? Shall the gods ask the consent of Edas before they select themselves a holy bride?"

"And thou, Nesta, art thou not a daughter of a race of kings? Is not the blood of Hu the Mighty in thy veins, the blood of heroes who feared nought, death least of all. Maiden, I tell thee the gods demand it. Only by thy death can the Romans be overthrown, and

4

Britain remain free. And behold the moon is even now in the sky, the hour of sacrifice is come."

Nesta the Fair flung her arms about her lover and kissed him.

"Farewell, my heart," she cried. "The gods prosper thee, and give thee a hero's death at last."

In another moment she was gone, and Edas, who knew the power of the Druids, fell on the ground and sobbed.

The wild warriors hurried on, and gathered in silence about the altar of sacrifice. There, between the upright stones, was bound the form of Nesta the Fair. About her were the white-robed Druids, and Caledon, the priest, stood near her on the altar.

The voice of Caledon rose, and the multitude drew their breaths to listen.

"To thee, Dread All Giver, Master of Life, and Death, we offer now the fairest maid in all the Isle of Britain. We give to thee our best beloved. Better far is it that she should become Thy bride than fall into the power of Roman ravishers. Deign to accept her blood as the price of British victory. May our spears be dyed in the blood of the Eagles, and may the Roman legions be swept away before the rush of our warriors, even as the leaves scatter before the wind."

So he chanted, and then, as the moonlight fell in a slanting beam upon the snow-white breasts of Nesta the Fair, he raised the golden knife, plunged it deep in the maiden's heart, and the spirit of the bride of Edas passed beyond the mountains to the Land of Rest.

Then Caledon turned to the warriors.

"Sons of Britain," he cried, "the Gods have accepted your sacrifice. Get ye to your spears. The air is thick with ghosts. The dead heroes have left their graves, and their spirits sail about the moor. Sing ye the songs of the heroes who died for Britain. For on the morrow the blood will flow like water, and it is well that ye know how to die. The victory will be as the gods decree, but end the battle as it may, see that the bards have a glorious song to sing of you, and let not the ghosts of your fathers be ashamed when they greet you in the after world."

Silently the warriors filed away, and, as they laid themselves to rest, the bards sang of glorious deeds. Thus passed the night, and on the morrow Edas the Chief, pale and heavy eyed with weeping, yet loyal and true to the land he loved, led his men to meet the Roman steel.

Now the British army was gathered upon the level summit of Coombs, which runs crescent shaped about the northern end of the valley, and commands the whole land beneath. One glance at this position convinced the skilful Roman leader of its impregnable character, and of the impossibility of taking it by direct assault. The rocks at the head of the basin-like vale presented an unscaleable barrier to the legions. The Roman general determined to seek some easier path to the summit. He moved his men to the right, and, working his way up the gentler slopes about Ludworth, reached the high ground which stands level with the crest of Coombs. Here, gathering his men in battle array, he prepared for a final assault upon the British line.

But the British finding that the Romans were not inclined to attempt the impossible task of scaling the rocks, and seeing no further advantage in maintaining their position, moved rapidly towards the west, and met the Romans on the Ludworth moor. Chanting their wild songs of battle, the warriors charged upon the Roman line. Again and again the warriors charged, but the legions stood firm, and the slaughter was horrible to see. The Britons fought for freedom, which was dearer to them than life, and few who went to battle that day returned home to tell the tale. It is said that the British army was annihilated, and certainly that was the last great fight between the Romans and the Britons which took place in this part of the country.

When the battle was ended the dead were buried in two great groups upon the field, and mighty cairns of stones were raised above their graves. These cairns still remain, and are probably the oldest monuments to British bravery in this district.

The chief Edas was one of the last to fall. He led charge after charge of his warriors, shouting his wild war cry, until at length, pierced by many blades, he fell far in front of the British. For a moment or so he lay as one dead. Then a glad smile spread over his face, and he sprang to his feet.

"Nesta, my beloved, I come. The gods are just. They will unite

6

us. We shall dwell together in the Land of Rest. Thus do I win my way to thy side."

So crying, he gripped his war hatchet, and, rushing full upon the line of Roman spears, slew until the soldiers made an end of him.

"That was truly a brave man," said the Roman general. "He could not have died a nobler death had he been a Roman." And having learned the story of the death of Nesta, he had the two bodies of the lovers buried in one grave. The Romans encamped in the neighbourhood, and at night were startled by a wild song which came from the battlefield. It was Caswallon the bard, who sang above the grave of Edas. And thus he sang.

"Now have the heroes gone beyond the veil of the Invisible, and the Land of Ghosts is thronged with the spirits of the brave."

"Edas, the son of Atli, led his warriors to join the hosts of their forefathers."

"Edas was of the blood of Hu the Mighty; he was glorious to look upon; fair was his countenance, even as the light of the morning; he was sturdy of stature as the oak; he was fleet of foot as the deer; his eye was as the eye of the eagle; men fell before him in the battle."

"He gave his heart to Nesta the Fair. She was the fairest maid in all Britain. The Gods had need of her."

"The Romans came, who are brave men. But the Britons are still braver. Every Briton is a warrior."

"Edas, the son of Atli, led his men to the battle. The battle raged, and the war song of Edas arose. Many brave men died, but the Britons still fought on. Edas, son of Atli, led the way; he led his warriors through the gates of death."

"The battle ended. The Romans won. But the Land of Ghosts welcomed the souls of Edas and his brave Britons."

"The men sleep beneath the cairns amid the heather. But their spirits sail upon the wind. And they shall watch over Britain until new heroes shall arise. And the fame of the Eagles shall grow dim before their fame, and Britain shall conquer, and shall be mightier than Rome."

Such was the song of Caswallon the bard.

It is said that at certain seasons of the year, when the moonlight falls upon the Coombs Rocks, the ghosts of the ancient heroes marshall on the battlefield, waving in phantom hands their phantom axes, as though ready for the coming of the Roman foe. Thus they keep eternal vigil over the wild land they loved of old.

Author's Note

The foregoing story is founded upon one of the earliest traditions of the neighbourhood, which states that a great battle between the ancient Britons and the Romans was fought upon the elevated ground in the vicinity of "Coombs Tor." Several writers of local history have included this battle in their accounts of actual events. Butterworth, the historian, gives an elaborate account of it in his description of the Coombs Cairns. He first mentions the conflict as having taken place between the Romans, "who were inspired by conquest and the thirst for military glory," and the Britons, who "fought for their country's independence"; and then he continues as follows: "Though the poet and other historians are silent upon the great engagement—for such I consider it to have been—yet two prodigious mounds, barrows or tumuli, at from a quarter to half a mile distant from each other, on the field of battle, remain to attest the magnitude and consequence of the action. I have been upon them both, and observed that they each consist of some hundred tons of stone heaped together in a circular or rather an oval form, covered with the effect of time. One of them has furze or dwarf gorse growing upon it, and I have seen cows in hot weather standing on their summits for the purpose of inhaling the cooling breezes." The same writer then goes on to record the erection of a Roman trophy stone at some short distance from the field, and also deduces evidence of the Druids once existing near.

In the neighbourhood of Coombs Rocks there are several relics of antiquity which are classed as Druidical. One of these, which consists of two upright stone pillars, rising from a massive stone base, is situated on Ludworth Moor. It is locally known as the "Robin Hood's Picking Rods," because Robin Hood and his men are said to have used it as a target for their arrows. But tradition states it to have been used by the Druids as an altar of sacrifice.

II

The Legend of Alman's Death

A Tale of Melandra Castle

WHEN the Roman general, Julius Agricola completed the subjugation of the Britons, he began to prepare for a permanent occupation of the country by erecting a series of strong military stations or forts throughout the entire kingdom. A number of these fortresses were built in Cheshire, Lancashire, and Derbyshire, and among the rest was Melandra Castle, erected on the banks of the river Etherow, in what is now known as the township of Gamesley. This fort was established about the end of the first century of the Christian era; it was well built and was of considerable size; moreover its importance was increased because it commanded the hill country north and east of Longdendale. It proved an admirable means of driving back the raids which the scattered hill-tribes were fond of making on the rich lands of the valley. The Romans originally called the fort "Zedrotalia," but, on account of its standing in a district where oak trees were plentiful, it came to be known by its present name. Melandra is said to be a Roman name derived from the Greek Melandryon, which signifies "The heart of oak," or "The heart in the oak," and is supposed to have reference to the fact that the forests of Longdendale were noted for their splendid oaks at the time when the Romans built their station.

The site of the Castle has been excavated during the years 1899-1905, and the result of this has been the securing of ample proof that Melandra was a station of great strength and importance. The foundations of walls of considerable thickness, with the masonry still solid and straight as on the day when it was laid, have been unearthed. Pieces of pottery, broken weapons, and coins have been found. There is also an inscribed stone containing the inscription—"Cohortis Primæ Frisianorum Centurio Valerius Vitalis." Dr. Watson, the eminent antiquary, translates this into "The Cohort of the First Frisians, Centurion Valerius Vitalis." The

9

Frisians were troops attached to the renowned Twentieth Legion—the "Valiant and Victorious"—and Valerius Vitalis is the only one of the Roman commanders whose name has been handed down.

Across the valley, some distance from Melandra, is a hill called Mouselow. This hill is supposed to have been a stronghold of the Ancient Britons. It forms a position of great natural strength, and was well adapted for military occupation in the days anterior to gunpowder and artillery. Several pre-historic weapons have been discovered near.

For a considerable time after the erection of Melandra Castle, the Roman garrison was much harassed by the activity of a chieftain who was encamped on Mouselow. This chief watched his opportunity, and rallying to his side the few fighting men of the Britons who were left, darted down on detached bands of the Roman soldiery, and left not one alive to tell the tale. Thus from the earliest days, it seemed fated that there was to be strife and enmity between the two strongholds. Even when the Romans had finally driven out the Britons, and razed the original building of Mouselow to the ground, the struggle did not cease; for after a time the legions were forced to leave the country, and no sooner had they turned their backs than the native chiefs were quarrelling over the spoils. One chief took possession of Melandra and became prince of that place, and a rival chief rebuilt the fort on Mouselow and took the title of Prince of Mouselow.

After a time came the Saxon invasion—bands of freebooters from the continent landed on these shores, and pillaged where they listed, some returning to their own land with the spoil they had won, others settling on the lands of the chiefs they had defeated and slain. Among the latter class was a Saxon chief named Alman—a brave, though ruthless warrior, who, after some fierce fighting put to death the Prince of Mouselow, and established himself in that mountain stronghold. Thereafter the country of Longdendale was never free from the depredations of this chief; his robber bands harassed the valleys, and no man's property was safe if it happened to attract the attention of the new Prince of Mouselow. He terrorised the native chiefs, who were nearly all reduced to a state of vassalage by him; indeed, of all those chiefs, the Prince of

Melandra alone maintained his former state of independence, and this principally because he was fortunate enough to hold a castle built by the Romans, which, as may be readily supposed, was the strongest fortress in that part of the country. Affairs were in this state when there occurred those incidents which form the substance of this legend.

Now Alman had set his heart upon winning the daughter of a neighbouring chief for his bride. She was named Ineld, and her father was the Lord of Woley—which at that time was a fair-sized town. He was a brave old man, but his forces had been defeated, and his territory ravaged by Alman's soldiers, so he was somewhat afraid of the Prince of Mouselow, and more than half inclined to bestow his daughter's hand upon Alman without ever consulting the girl's wishes at all.

But it chanced that Ineld had views of her own upon the subject, and Alman and his robber ways were not to her liking. She had heard things of Alman and his doings which made the blood run cold.

One day there had come to her father's gate an old woman, who craved an audience of the chief.

"Why are thine eyes so heavy with mourning?" asked the Lord of Woley. And the old dame made answer:

"O Chief, I am a widow, and the only stay and comfort of my old age was my son—an only child. He kept me from beggary and want. He loved a maiden, and hoped shortly to make her his wife, and even to-day they talked together by the roadside. But it chanced that the Prince of Mouselow rode by with his retinue, and, happening to catch sight of the maid, he ordered his guards to seize her and carry her to the castle. My son interfered, and in an instant the Prince of Mouselow slew him with his own hand. And now, O chief, I cry aloud to thee for justice."

And another day one of her father's serfs had come in weeping.

"My lord," he cried, "I am heavy of heart. I have suffered a great wrong, and I look to thee for redress. My farm, as thou knowest, is on the boundary of the Prince of Mouselow's territory, and to-day, in my absence, his men came and carried off my cattle and much store of corn. Also, when my wife, who is very fair, remonstrated with them, they seized her and carried her away to their prince, and my little child they slew with the sword."

ROMAN COINS, BRICKS, AND TILES, FOUND AT MELANDRA CASTLE

These things had Ineld heard, and they in no way predisposed her in favour of Alman, nor did the appearance of the chief when he came a-wooing, alter her first opinions of him. He was a rough, boisterous man, who drank deep, and swore loud oaths—fine and handsome of outward appearance, but a man lacking that refinement which most women prefer to see in men.

Having disclosed his intention to the Lord of Woley, Alman made his way to the fair Ineld's side, but so used was he to wooing by force that he could not even now altogether rid himself of his blunt, repulsive manner.

"Ah, my May," cried he, stealing behind the maid, and flinging his arm roughly about her waist, "one kiss from those rosy lipe of thine, and then we will talk of love."

12

He laughed as the startled Ineld struggled to free herself from his grasp, but a scowl of anger swept over his face as, with her little hand, she struck him heavily upon the coarse lips which he had thrust near her face.

Then he laughed again, and even swore.

"By Woden," said he, "but you are a fit wife for any chief. Little spitfire—but I like such play. Trust me, I love thee none the less for that blow. Some day I will tame thee, and then, by the gods, we shall make a mighty pair."

"Never," cried Ineld fiercely.

And, breaking away, she ran to the mansion, and hid herself in the women's quarters, where even Alman dared not follow.

That day the Prince of Mouselow rode away immensely pleased with himself; he loved to see a maid full of fight, so he said, and he promised himself that Ineld should love him by and by. But the days went past, and do what he would, he could never persuade the maiden to grant him an interview alone.

His spirit chafed at the prolonged delay, and at length he determined upon bolder measures. He lay in wait in the woodland near the home of Ineld, and in due course his patient waiting was rewarded. The fair maiden appeared, and, first looking timidly around, as though to make sure she was unobserved, made her way through the glade to a spot near a fern-covered spring.

Alman chuckled to himself with glee, and silently he kept pace with the maiden, although remaining concealed the while.

When Ineld stopped, and showed unmistakable signs of going no further, the Prince of Mouselow emerged from the undergrowth behind which he had been hidden, and, with a laugh of triumph, stood before her.

"Now, my little vixen," said he, "I have won you at last. Maids so coy as you must be wooed in rough fashion. And, once inside my mountain fortress, I doubt not your consent to wed Alman will soon be forthcoming."

So saying, he made to carry her to the spot where his steed was tethered, for he would win his bride by force, even as he had won his wealth and lands.

13

Ineld screamed shrilly in terror, and the Prince clapped his rough hand upon her lips to stifle the cries.

"Cease such idle wailing," said he. "The wood is deserted, no one can hear, nor would it greatly matter if they could. I hold thee now, and no man in all the land shall rob me of my prize."

"Be not so sure of that," said a voice at his shoulder, so suddenly and unexpectedly that Alman dropped the girl, who immediately, with a joyful cry, sprang to the side of the new comer.

"Lewin—sweetheart," cried she—then could say no more by reason of the caress which her deliverer bestowed upon her.

"Ah," cried Alman—a light breaking on him, as he recognised the youthful Lewin, Prince of Melandra. "So 'tis a lover's tryst I have marred by my presence. Well, let us see who is the better man—Lewin or Alman, and the winner takes the maid."

He loosened the short axe at his side, and, without pause, rushed on Lewin, waving the weapon aloft. Scarce had the youth time to thrust the maid behind him and draw his blade when the axe fell; but the sword of Lewin was swift to parry, and at the same instant he sprang aside. The axe missed him by a hairsbreadth, but the sword was shattered by the stroke, and the Prince of Melandra stood weaponless—at the mercy of Alman.

The Prince of Mouselow laughed, and again raised his axe to make an end, but Lewin, disdaining to fly, faced him calmly, awaiting death without a tremour. His cool and gallant bearing touched the fierce robber, and he dropped his arm.

"I could slay thee easily," said he, "but I soil not my fame so. Thou art a brave man, and above all the chiefs about, hast hitherto opposed me with credit to thyself. I give thee thy life—the maiden goes with me. But this chance I give thee. Rally thy men and meet me now in battle array—Melandra against Mouselow, and we will fight for a noble prize—the lordship of all the land of Longdendale, and the fair Ineld for a queen. Thou may'st trust me. The maid stays in my keeping, but I touch her not until the battle has been fought and won."

Lewin advanced and took the hand of Alman.

"I trust thee, Prince," said he. "'Tis a noble act. Get thee to

14

INSCRIBED ROMAN STONE FOUND AT MELANDRA CASTLE

thy stronghold with the maiden, for soon the axe of Lewin will be knocking at thy door."

Then, turning to the trembling girl, he whispered:

"Fear not, Ineld, I come quickly. Ere another hour is passed the war-song of Lewin will echo through the hills."

Then he was gone.

An hour later Alman stood on the rampart of Mouselow, and gazed in the direction of Melandra. The warrior by his side pointed to a dancing light which played upon the distant fields and seemed to move on Mouselow. It was the sunlight reflected from a host of shields and spears.

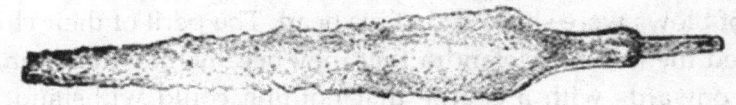

PREHISTORIC SPEAR HEAD FOUND NEAR MOUSELOW CASTLE

"They come, my lord," said he. And Alman answered:

"This Lewin keeps his word. The fight will be such as a soldier loves. Now get to your arms."

The Prince of Mouselow watched the approach of the foe with gladness. Rude and tyrannous though he might be, he was yet a brave man, and asked for nothing better than a worthy foe and a fair field. It mattered little to him if death came in the conflict. His fathers had all died fighting, and he, too, longed to die in the thick

15

of the fray. He loved fighting for fighting's sake, and in the lust for the conflict he even forgot the fair Ineld—the prize for which he fought. Placing himself at the head of his men, he led them out of the fort, and soon the two forces were in touch with each other. The Prince of Melandra was at the head of his own troops, and as the two armies closed he gave forth his war shout and called upon his men to charge. The warriors clashed their axes and shields together, and cried aloud:

"Lewin we will follow thee to death. Lead on!"

And thus the great fight begun.

The battle lasted through the day, and it seemed almost certain that the superior force of the Prince of Mouselow would win. But the men of Melandra fought like heroes; they stubbornly maintained their ground, and, as the day passed, the battle was still undecided.

Throughout the combat Lewin seemed to bear a charmed life. He was ever in the thick of battle, and where his axe descended there death reigned in the foemen's ranks. But towards the evening he realised that his rapidly thinning ranks were in danger of being enveloped by the greater number of the foe, and that if the battle was to be saved, it would require a superhuman effort.

Then, knowing that where he led his men would surely follow, he raised his war shout, and, with a mighty rush, charged single-handed on the foe. He was surrounded in an instant, and a score of blows were showered at his head. The peril of their chief so incensed the men of Melandra that they became like madmen, and swept onwards with a charge that nothing could withstand. This was exactly what Lewin had looked for, and, hoping to render the effect of the charge doubly sure, he still pushed on, making for the standard where Alman fought.

The Prince of Mouselow rallied his men about him, and, shoulder to shoulder, they stood to repel the onslaught. But the rush of Lewin was too fierce, the men of Mouselow were scattered like chaff, and Alman himself fell pierced by a score of blades.

With the fall of Alman the battle ended, his men fled from the field, and their dying chief turned and laughed as he watched them fly.

16

"They run," said he—"the dogs. And yet—they fought bravely. Well, let them run. Ho. Lewin, the day is thine. Ineld is thine, and I—I die. Tell her I died as a brave man should—face to the foe. Valhalla calls me. Lewin, farewell."

THE PRINCESS INELD

So he died.

The old chronicle tells us that he died as the sun set, and his spirit passed away with the dying beams to the eternal land of rest. It is said that so keen was the conflict, and so great was the bloodshed, that one part of the battlefield was afterwards termed Redgate in perpetual commemoration of the day. The spot whereon Alman died was called Almansdeath, a name it still retains.

Author's Note

There are many traditions which speak of the fierce encounters between the forces of Melandra and Mouselow. They are, however, extremely vague, and it is difficult to say whether the story of Alman refers to a battle between the Romans and the

Britons, or a struggle of the later Saxon period. For the purpose of this narrative I have adopted the latter date. It may be added that Melandra has been a favourite theme with local writers. The following fragments from the pen of Thomas Barlow, the Longdendale poet, will serve as illustrations of the way in which the "castle" has been the subject of song and romance.

And well I loved the roaring flood—
The wind, when whistling through the wood,
Below where once Melandra stood,
With turrets high;
And often stray'd at eve, to brood
On days gone by;

In which, traditions old declare,
Melandra flourish'd, free and fair,
And glisten'd in the morning air,
Anent the sun;
Ere Time, who swept the ruins bare,
His freaks begun.

When lordly knight, at dawn of day,
Led forth his train—a proud array
Of stalwart warriors blithe and gay
With martial fire;
Whose arms upheld the feudal sway
Of knight and squire.

When martial music could entrance,
And prompt the love inspiring glance,
Till knights and ladies would advance,
Quick-step or slow;
In halls where hung the sword and lance,
And good yew bow.

In fancy oft I saw the throng,
And heard the aged minstrel's song,

18

As, softly sweet, he did prolong,
His tender strain;
With themes of love or war his tongue
Could audience gain.

When deeds of arms his song would claim,
He sang Melandra's knightly fame,
And hung with reverence on the name
His chieftain bore,
Till tears reveal'd the ardent flame
That fired his lore.

III

King Arthur's Adventure

ARTHUR, son of Uthyr, Pendragon of Great Britain, organised that high order of Christian chivalry, commonly known as the knighthood of the Round Table. The companions of this Order bound themselves by oath to oppose the progress of paganism, to be loyal to the British throne, to fight—not for self-glory, but for the redressing of human wrong, to protect the defenceless, to show mercy to the fallen, to honour womanhood, and never to turn their backs upon a foe in battle.

It is said that God raised up King Arthur that he might render Britain free, drive out the heathen, purify his realm, and spread Christ among men. For this purpose, the Lady of the Lake, "clothed in white samite, mystic, wonderful," gave to the king the huge cross-hilted sword, "Excalibur," which was forged beneath the sea, whose blade was so bright that men were blinded by it, and before whose sweep no man might stand. With this blade, Arthur led his knighthood, and in twelve great battles overcame the Saxon heathen hordes. It is said that four of these great victories of the young Pendragon were fought in Lancashire, and that after the battles the knights of the Round Table rode through the country, redressing the wrongs of the people, and putting tyrants to the sword.

At this time there were great castles on the hills of Longdendale, and in one of these strongholds dwelt a cruel and treacherous knight of gigantic stature and enormous strength. On account of his many cruelties he was known as Sir Terrible. His fortress was built upon a commanding eminence; it was defended by ramparts surmounted by massive towers of stone, and was so strong a place that it had never yet been taken by a foe.

Sir Terrible was not married, though he was now in the prime of life. It was said that no woman would mate with him, so black were his deeds. Strange tales were told of his love passages, and many a country maiden had mysteriously disappeared. Rumour said that the knight carried off the maidens to his dreadful dwelling under cover of the darkness, and it was certain that when morning came, the cottage of each victim was found in ashes, and the dead bodies of the kinsfolk lay around. No trace of the maids could be found, and they were never seen again, though shrieks and cries of agony floated on the air from the direction of the castle walls.

Now King Arthur held Court after one of his great victories, which he won near Wigan, and to him flocked the people from far and near, laying their grievances before the King, and beseeching help at his hands. Among the rest came an old dame from Longdendale, who wept bitterly as she told her story, bewailing the loss of the fairest maid in all Cheshire. For it seemed that the maiden was the old dame's grandchild, that they two lived in a lonely spot in the valley of Longdendale, that Sir Terrible had become enamoured of the maid, and had carried her to his castle, where he kept her a prisoner, neither suffering her to go out, nor yet anyone to hold converse with her. Also he had slain two noble knight-errants to whom the dame had told her tale, and who had chivalrously sought to rescue the maiden.

It was towards the close of the day when the old dame told her story, for there had been a large attendance of petitioners to see the King; moreover all the knights had left the court on some quest or other in keeping with their oaths as members of the Round Table. But when the King heard of the cruelty of Sir Terrible, he rose at once, the gentle look passed from his face, and in its place gleamed the determined light of battle. He donned his war-gear, and buckled the great sword "Excalibur" to his side. Then, accompanied only by a young squire, and dressed only as a simple knight, he rode away towards Longdendale.

The King rested for the night at the hut of a poor peasant, from whom he gleaned tidings of many fresh cruelties of Sir Terrible. Early in the morning he set out and soon came in sight of the Castle.

Now, as they rode, the young squire had been silent. But when the Castle towers hove in sight he spoke to the King.

"My liege," said he, "My father was a knight at the court of

21

Uthyr Pendragon, and was esteemed meet company for brave men. I, his son, have not yet done a deed worthy of mine ancestry. Grant, I pray, that this quest be mine to follow. 'Tis true I am untried, and the foe is strong, yet the cause is just, and, mayhap, God will nerve my arm."

So he pleaded, for he desired above all else the chance to do some Christian deed that might win for him the fellowship of the Round Table.

After much persuasion the king at last granted him his prayer, and the Squire rode with a glad heart to the castle gate, while Arthur hid himself among the trees.

Reaching the gate, the squire thundered at it with his lance, and then drew back to wait. In answer to his knocking, the knight Sir Terrible appeared, ready mounted, armed with lance and sword.

"Villain and treacherous knight," cried the squire. "How darest thou abduct innocent and defenceless maidens, whom all thy Order are bound to protect, keeping them as slaves within thy castle? I am come to make thee rue this foul insult to the order of our good King Arthur; for thy cruelties are a stain upon the honour of his knighthood, and a blotch upon the fair fame of his kingdom."

"Thou discourteous churl," answered Sir Terrible. "Do but lead on to yon level piece of green, and I will first meet thee in fair fight, and then send thy carcase to thy base born king."

Now the squire, used to the honour of noble knights, turned to ride to the greensward indicated, but no sooner was his back turned than the treacherous Sir Terrible, couching his lance, drove at him between the shoulders, striking him so fierce a blow that the squire fell senseless to the ground.

Then the knight laughed loudly, and would have hacked off the head of his fallen foe, had not the king, who was now dismounted, stepped from the shelter of the trees, and stood above the prostrate squire.

"Thou cruel traitor," cried the king. "That foul stroke shall cost thee thy life. Never have I seen a blow more foul."

On seeing this new foe, Sir Terrible—who did not recognise the king—again couched his lance, and, without waiting to give his opponent chance to mount, and meet him in fair combat, charged down upon the king.

"A COUNTRY MAID OF LONGDENDALE"

But Arthur stood calm and firm, and drawing Excalibur from its sheath, he stepped aside as the horseman charged, and smote with all his might. The blow cut clean through the lance close to the haft, and falling on the steed, brought it to the ground. Instantly the knight sprang up in terror.

"Now I know thee," he cried. "Thou art Arthur Pendragon. No sword save the brand Excalibur could have struck so great a blow as that."

"Thou speakest truly," answered the king. "I am indeed Pendragon."

Then the coward knight turned to fly, for well he knew that none might stand before Excalibur and live.

But the king stepped forward. He raised the great sword aloft. The blade flashed in the sunlight. It cut clean through the iron helm, and the head of Sir Terrible rolled on the sward.

After slaying the tyrant—so the story tells us—King Arthur

23

restored the squire, who was merely wounded, and then the two, mounting their steeds, rode up to the castle gates. The king rode in front, and at his saddle bow there hung the bloody head of the dead tyrant.

Arthur raised his lance, and with it thundered on the outer gate.

"Ho! warder," cried the king, "open instantly!"

But the warder made answer—

"Who art thou who knockest so loudly? Know that I hold the castle for Sir Terrible, and that I open only when my master comes."

At which the king laughed.

"Then open hastily," said he, "for thy master is here even now."

And swinging his arms, he hurled the gory head of the traitor knight over the iron spikes of the gate, so that it fell with a thud at the feet of the warder. The terrified fellow shrieked and fled, and his cries rang through the castle, causing the men-at-arms to grasp their weapons and stand at attention.

By this time the king was hammering loudly at the gate— great blows that shook the stout oaken portal so that it trembled in its sockets, and threatened to fall into splinters.

"By my troth," cried the captain of the men-at-arms, "but 'tis a mighty arm which deals such blows. No wonder our master fell before it."

Then, leaning over the rampart, he called aloud:

"Ho! there without. Who art thou who makest such a din; and what is thy business?"

Then Arthur made answer:

"I am the king,"

Whereupon the men were overcome with fear, and casting aside their weapons, they opened the gate, and surrendered the castle to King Arthur. The king ordered all the captives to be set at liberty, and this was immediately done, the long procession of unfortunate victims of the cruelty of Sir Terrible passing before the king, each one blessing him for having wrought their deliverance.

Last of all came the maiden whose rescue had been the immediate cause of the king's visit to Longdendale. She was wondrously beautiful, and as she stood before him, Arthur was so struck by her good looks that he could not refrain from passing knightly compliments.

"Such beauty as thine," said he, "would best befit a court. 'Tis wasted in these wilds. Thou shalt have a place among the maidens who wait upon the Queen."

But the maiden answered:

"If it please thee, sire, I would stay in fair Longdendale. I am but a country maiden. I love the free life of these hills and valleys; and at thy court I should be but as a wild bird in a cage."

Whereupon the king, noticing her earnest look of supplication, smilingly bent his head, and suffered her to depart.

Now the rest of the tale is soon told. The king bestowed the castle and the lands of the dead Sir Terrible, upon the young squire who had accompanied him, and whom he now made into a knight.

And then great changes took place in that part of Longdendale. Instead of being looked upon with dread by all the people of the countryside, the castle came to be regarded as the seat of a protecting power, to whose lord the poor might look for succour in time of need, and for justice in all seasons.

And perhaps the greatest change of all took place in the maiden who had been rescued from the clutches of Sir Terrible by King Arthur and his squire. Formerly she had trembled at the very name of the lord of the castle, and had witnessed his approach with a terror as great as that which causes the timid to shrink from death. But now she shrank from his approach no longer, there were even whispers that she kept tryst with the new lord; and at length there arrived a day when the young knight came in state, and carried her to the castle—a willing captive—where, in the presence of the king, they were made man and wife. The two lived long and happily together, trusted by the king, respected by their equals, and beloved by all who were beneath them in station. The knight won great renown as a warrior, so much so that evil-disposed men feared to meet him, and during his lifetime, although there were wars in other parts of the kingdom, the land of Longdendale enjoyed peace.

In due time the knight and his lady had several fine sons,

who grew up after the pattern of the king, and long maintained the fair fame of Arthur Pendragon in Longdendale, even in days after the good king had passed from life, to sail in the black barge with the three Queens, to Avilion, the Isle of Rest.

Author's Note

Concerning the connection of King Arthur with Longdendale, it may be of interest to mention that Bernard Robinson, in his "History of Longdendale," writes thus:—"Traditions speak of castles and kings, and great bloody battles fought along the hills—traditions of the times of Aurelius Ambrosius, and King Arthur, that have come

"Floating down the tide of years' mantled in mystery."

I may further add that it is not surprising to find Longdendale associated by tradition with the great hero of English romance. Several great battles of King Arthur are said to have been fought in Lancashire and Cheshire, and the former county is very closely linked with the chief of the knights of the Round Table. The name Lancashire is said to mean "Lancelot's Shire." Lancelot of the Lake is reputed to have been monarch or ruler of this county.

IV

The Legend of War Hill

IT was early autumn of the year 1138, and the Valley of Longdendale was a vast tract of desolation. True, the trees were still decked with verdure, and the mellow tint of autumn clothed nature with a lovely garb. The streams still murmured with silvery splashes as they wandered through the woodland, and the birds warbled among the branches. In all this the valley was as of old— lovely, radiant, fair. But the song of the reaper was never heard; the fields were tangled and untilled, the instruments of husbandry were destroyed or abandoned, and a grievous famine reigned. For the demon of war was abroad, and the blight of his shadow had fallen on the fair Cheshire vale.

King Stephen was seated on the throne which he had won by violence. As he had usurped the sovereign power without the pretence of a title, he was necessitated to tolerate in others, the same violence to which he himself had been beholden for his crown. Even in time of peace the nobles made sad havoc with the property of the people, but now that war was in the land, and the forces of the Lady Matilda, King Henry's child, sought to drive the usurper from the throne,—now, indeed, the castles poured forth bands of licensed robbers, and the homesteads of Longdendale were burned, the people driven to the woods, and the flocks and herds of the yeomen were confiscated.

Had the reader been privileged to wander through the woodland glades near Mottram, he would, maybe, have seen a group of fugitives bargaining with a sturdy forester for leave to shelter themselves in the depths of the forest, without fear of molestation.

"Thou hast known me all my life," said the leader of the party, "for a patient, God-fearing, and faithful husbandman. I have ever kept the forest laws, and seek not to work harm therein even now. But Mottram town is no place for me, for all my poor belongings have been seized by the King's men, and my hut has

27

been burned to the ground. And but yesterday there came a party of the other side, and their leader had me up, and soundly thrashed me, because he said I helped the King, and was disloyal to the Princess. Helped the King, forsooth, when the King helped himself to all I had, and turned me out o' doors to shift for myself."

"And I," quoth another, "come from Tingetvisie (Tintwistle), and there the townsfolk are so scared they dare not seek their beds at night. Nothing have I left to call my own, not even arms with which to protect myself. Truly the forest is a heaven to all such poor people as we."

"Well, well," grumbled the bluff forester, "get into the woods and hide yourselves, but play not with the deer at your peril. A pest on these troubles. I would the great folk would settle their differences themselves, and allow the poor to live in peace. Get off, I say, and hide yourselves. Steer clear of both King's men and Queen's men, and be damned to both sides."

So saying he went on his way whistling, and the fugitives hastily left the path, and were soon lost from view in the undergrowth. There, like beasts of the forest, they lay by day, and emerged when the night fell, to pick up such scraps of food as were to be had by the way. Little wonder there were robbers on the roads in those times.

Days passed on, and the wanderers in the woods beheld parties of rovers, riding with lance and sword, now north, now south, as the tide of war ebbed and flowed. Rumours had reached them of an invasion of the Scots under King David, and following the rumours came bands of wild Highland men, who laid waste with fire and sword what little the robber-bands of the English knighthood had spared. The King of Scotland came south to aid his niece, the Princess Matilda, and with the appearance of his army on this side the border, the nobles who favoured the Princess arose. There was a mustering of all the able-bodied men of the Vale of Longdendale, and, glad to strike a blow to bring the state of tumult to an end, the men took sides.

"Hast thou heard the news?" asked one fugitive of another.

"To what news dost thou refer, good man?" was the reply. "Is it more of evil?"

"Nay, that is as thou listest," was the answer. "'Tis said the King of Scots rides hither with a great following of men at arms, and that King Stephen's forces muster for the combat. In that case there may be a great struggle toward, and now, maybe, we shall see the ending of all this strife and misery."

"In that case, good man, methinks I will strike a blow for one side, so that the matter may indeed be ended."

"On what side art thou?"

"I am for the Princess."

"And I for King Stephen."

"Then we are enemies, but I bear thee no ill-will. Mayhap we shall meet again in the battle."

"Maybe. At least it will be better than starving in the woods. I wish thee a good-morrow."

"And I thee. Farewell."

Upon which the speakers went their several ways to arrange themselves beneath the banners of the cause they favoured.

Soon there was a fair mustering of each faction, and with the trains of knights, who came from north and south, the rival forces grew from companies into armies. King Stephen sent a great body of horse and foot to strengthen the array of those who fought beneath his banner, whilst stray bands of Highland men swelled the ranks of the warriors of Matilda.

Now the chief forester of Longdendale was a man with a kind heart, and to all those civil and respectable folk who took to the woods for a refuge, he showed such toleration and care as his position allowed; only upon the idle, thieves, and evildoers, was his anger bestowed. It was no new thing for him to meet with fugitives—particularly women—seeking shelter in the forest, and, accordingly, he gave little heed to a small band of riders in which were several females, who entered the forest of Longdendale upon a certain evening just before the hour of sunset.

"Another band of fugitives," said he. "Poor souls; God have mercy on them."

He would have passed on his way had not one of the band—a sturdy-looking young man, dressed in plain russet garb—thus accosted him:

29

"Ho there, fellow," cried the youth. "Come thou hither, for I would have a word with thee."

The tone in which the words were spoken was commanding, and to the forester it sounded insolent.

For answer he turned, and looking the horseman straight in the face said:

"Have a care, knave, what words thou usest to thy betters, or thou art likely to rue such speeches as that."

The young man frowned, and, raising a light riding whip, made as though he would strike the forester. But the latter brought into position a stout oak staff which he carried, and, advancing boldly, said in a threatening voice:

"Take advice from an older man, and drop thy paltry weapon. Otherwise I shall be put to the necessity of cracking thy pate. One blast of this horn now dangling at my side will speedily summon some of the stoutest lads in Cheshire, and thou and thy followers will ere long be dangling from the nearest tree."

So saying, the bold forester blew upon his horn, and scarcely had the echoes died away ere five stalwart men clad in green, each armed with yew-bow and quiver, and long knives at their girdle, burst from the thickets and ranged themselves by the forester's side.

What the newcomers would have done with the old forester at their head, it is difficult to say; but a diversion was created by one of the female riders, chiding the horseman who had first spoken.

"Thou art over-hasty, and even rude," said she; "where is thy discernment. Seest thou not that these men are honest, and wouldst thou set them against us?".

Then, advancing alone, she bent in her saddle, and whispered something to the forester. The old man started, gazed at the speaker, for a moment, then doffed his cap, and bowed low. Next turning to the five who stood behind him, he cried:

"Uncover, and on your knees. It is the Queen."

The Royal Matilda—for she it was, thus driven with her infant son, Henry, and a few faithful followers, to adopt the disguise of poor travellers, and to seek for a place of refuge until the coming battle should decide her fate—smiled graciously upon the old man and his companions.

"Methinks there is a likeness in all your faces," said she. "Are these thy sons?"

"They are my sons," answered the forester; "and withal thy loyal subjects, gracious lady, ready to give their lives for thee and thine."

After a few further passages of speech, the chief forester led the way to his own dwelling—which was a strongly built and well concealed place, where, attended by his good wife, the Queen might rest secure until the battle had been fought and won.

Meanwhile the forester and his sons donned their war-gear, and when the time was ripe they took their stand with the rest of those who fought beneath the banner of the Queen.

It was in the gray dawning of an autumn day when the two armies met. The battle was fought on a hill in the Mottram township, where the ancient Church of Mottram now stands. But there was no sacred building there on that gray morning of long ago, when the clashing of arms awoke the echoes, and the air was heavy with the shrieks of dying men.

The army of Matilda was posted on the hill. Their position was strong and commanding. From it they could note the approach of the foe, and fight him with advantage. In the midst of their array rose the standard of the Princess—the royal banner of the great Henry—and by its side the bonnie flag of Scotland floated in the breeze.

As the gray light broke from the east, the watchers on the hill beheld the first line of Stephen's forces emerge from the woods. The King's army was a mighty host, the bright spears gleamed in the light of dawn, and the archers carried great quivers full of deadly goose-tipped shafts.

The royal force came on, and the leading ranks broke into a battle-chant as they neared the hill foot, and bent to meet the slope. The archers winged their shafts, the axes, bills, and pikes advanced; a rain of arrows beat whistling from the ranks upon the hill, and the great fight commenced.

Bit by bit the soldiers of Stephen advanced up the hill. They left many dead upon the slopes, but still the host went on. The army of Matilda hung thick and massive upon the crest, and waited with unbroken front for the closing of the foe; they rained down their flights of arrows, but kept their ranks unbroken, with bristling rows of pikes in front.

At length the advancing host drew near. The foremost men rushed bravely on, they clutched the wall of pikes with their hands, and strove to hew a way to victory. But the arrows fell among them, dealing death in full measure, and the brave men fell. Others took their places, and again the goose-shafts flew.

Now the advancing army remembered the trick of Norman William on the field of Senlac. At a given signal they turned and fled in apparent confusion. With a wild yell the unwary Highland men broke from their post upon the summit, and charged down to slay. Then, swift as lightning, the warriors of Stephen turned. Their archers met the onrush of the pursuers with a staggering volley of shafts. The pikes and bills charged up the slope. The axes hacked the brawny Scots, and the broken ranks upon the hill, opening wider yet to receive their retreating comrades, let in the charging body of the foe. After that there was a mingled mass of slaying men about the summit. The hosts of King Stephen girt the hill round, so that there was no escape for the men who stood upon it. Death was everywhere, death for the victors and the vanquished; for the soldiers of the Princess died as soldiers should, and they slew great numbers of the foe.

MOTTRAM CHURCH AND THE WAR HILL, THE SITE OF THE BATTLE MENTIONED IN THE LEGEND

That was the last stand for the Princess Matilda in that part of Cheshire, and the old chronicles say that the blood shed in the battle ran in a stream down the slopes, and formed a great pool at the foot of the hill.

As the gray of the morrow's dawn fell upon the scene of battle, the pale light fell also upon a group of living beings, who stood upon the summit of the hill among the hosts of the dead.

Matilda, the Queen, was there—beaten and dismayed, since all hope was lost. The chief forester of Longdendale stood there also, and he, too, sighed, as one whose heart is broken—he had just been groping among the corpses, and had found what he sought.

"Are thy fears well founded?" asked Matilda, anxiously.

The old man pointed to the inert forms of five dead men.

"They were all I had—and I am an old man. Now they are gone, my very name must perish."

The royal lady looked at him for a moment, her whole being trembling with grief.

"My heart is broken," she said. "Yet what is my loss to thine?"

The old man took her hand, and kissed it.

"I am a loyal man—and an Englishman. I gave them freely to the cause of my Queen. Who am I that I should complain?"

Royal lady and lowly-born forester gazed into each other's eyes for a brief space—their looks conveying thoughts which were too sacred for words—and then the Queen's train moved down the hill, and the old man was left alone—alone with his sorrow and his dead.

The world is full of changes, and ever on the heels of war comes the angel form of peace. Men called the hill whereon the battle had been fought Warhill, and in after days the builders raised the sacred pile of Mottram Church, where the soldiers of Matilda and Stephen fought and died.

Author's Note

According to an old Longdendale tradition, the War Hill, Mottram, is the site of a battle which was fought in the twelfth century between the forces of the Princess Matilda and King Stephen.

33

V

Sir Ro of Staley Hall

THERE was a noble gathering in the great banqueting room of Staley Hall, on that memorable morning when Sir Ro or Ralph de Stavelegh entertained his guests for the last time ere he set sail for the Holy Land. The message of war had been sent through all merrie England, and many of the Cheshire knights were leaving their homes, their wide and pleasant meadows, and their dear wives and children, to engage in the stern conflict of the great Crusade. Sir Ro, of Staley, was one of the first to offer his sword in the holy cause. He was a brave knight, born of a war-like ancestry, and desirous above all things to risk his life in so sacred a war. And now he had called together his friends and neighbours, that they might feast once more in the old banqueting hall, and pledge themselves as true and leal comrades before the knight said farewell.

There were many brave knights and squires, many noble dames and fair maidens, seated about that hospitable board. But the lovliest of all women gathered there was the young lady of Staley, and the handsomest of men in that goodly company was the warrior knight, Sir Ro.

The feasting went on well into the night. In the minstrels' gallery there were harpers who harped of war, and bards who sang of heroes' deeds and victory. The music was wild and glorious; it lured men to war, it breathed the spirit of strife, it lured the love of maidens to the man who wielded axe and sword. When the music ceased there were speeches made by the knights, and good wishes expressed, and the words of friendship passed.

Then the Knight of Staley rose to bid farewell. He spoke of the true comradeship between his guests and himself. He begged them to see that no enemy laid waste his fair domain while he was distant at the war. By every tie of friendship, he prayed them to protect well his dear lady should ever the need arise. Then, turning to his wife, he asked that she should hand her wedding ring to him,

34

and the lady complied. Holding up the ring, and in sight of all the guests, Sir Ro next snapped the golden circlet in twain, and, restoring one half to his spouse, he placed the other against his heart, swearing by that token to be a true lover and husband until death. On her part, the lady made a like vow, and thus, before all that noble company, they pledged again eternal troth.

On the morrow, with many bitter tears at the pain of the parting, with many tender kisses and protestations of fidelity, Sir Ro and his lady parted—the lady to her lonely bower, the knight to his ship, his journey, and the war.

Sir Ro sailed the seas in company with many other English knights and men-at-arms. They marched across the great desert, suffering many privations, often being in peril of death by the wilderness, and at other times endangered by the craft and might of the foe. They fought many battles, winning great glory for the Christian arms, and putting numbers of the Saracens to death. In all the fighting Sir Ro of Staley played a great part. He was ever in the thickest of the battle, his helm bore the marks and dints of many blows, his breast was scarred with wounds, his sword dulled with hacking, his axe chipped with striking. Wherever he rode the foe fell like hail beaten by the wind. They were powerless before him; death came to them with the falling of his brand; and before his arm multitudes of heathen bit the dust.

"IN THE MINSTRELS' GALLERY"

At length befell an evil day for the Christian army. Sir Ro was captured by a cunning strategy of the foe, and, bound hand and foot, was carried off to a Saracen town. There, stripped of his knightly raiment, and dressed in the poor garb of a palmer, he was cast into a filthy and dark dungeon, and there left to pine and die.

For long dreary months did the brave knight suffer this cruel captivity without a murmur or complaint. His cheeks grew white, his limbs thin, his frame was wasted; the palmer's dress hung loose about his figure. None would have recognised in that feeble prisoner the once gay and handsome lord of Staley Hall.

One night Sir Ro fell into a troubled sleep, in which he dreamed some horrid dream. It seemed that some great evil threatened his wife and kindred at home—an evil which he had no power to avert. So vivid was the dream that, on awakening, the force of his anguish was such as to cause his frame to tremble and his heart to languish with despair. But, like a good Christian knight, he fell upon his knees and poured forth his soul in earnest prayer to God, asking his Heavenly Father to succour his wife in the hour of peril, and, by some means—if it were His will—to restore him to his home.

Having thus prayed, a calm fell upon the knight, and, repeating the Saviour's prayer, he laid himself upon his couch, and fell into a gentle sleep.

Sir Ro awoke with a start. It seemed as though a bright light from heaven blinded him. There was a warmth as of living fire about him. All the cell seemed a-flame. Then his full senses came, and he leaped and cried aloud for joy.

There in front of him was the fairest scene in all the world.

Gone was the cold damp cell, gone the poisonous atmosphere of the dungeon, gone were the iron fetters, his strength had returned to him, and lo!—before him, shining fair in the summer sunlight, rich in the fulsome melody of singing birds, was a fair English landscape, and beyond it his own ancestral hall of Staley.

God had heard his prayer. By His own Almighty working he had bridged time and space, and Sir Ro was safe again at his old English home.

36

"A miracle, a miracle!" exclaimed the knight. And, like a good Christian, he fell upon his knees, and gave thanks to God.

When he arose Sir Ro passed along the soft and level sward of green until he came to the hall door. There he knocked long and loud. The warder who answered the knocking, failed to recognise the knight.

"Who knocks so long and loudly?" asked the warder, peering curiously at the palmer. "For a holy man, friend, methinks thou hast a mighty powerful stroke."

This greeting reminded Sir Ro that he was no longer dressed as a knight, but in the garb of a palmer, and that he had best put off knightly ways unless he wished to be discovered, so, in a feigned voice, he answered:

"I am a humble palmer, hungry and footsore, and I crave a meal and leave to rest awhile. All of which I pray ye grant for Christ Jesu's sake."

"Well, well," said the warder, somewhat mollified by the penitent tone of his visitor, "of a truth thou lookest woe-begone and travel-stained. Come thou within and eat and drink, and then, perchance, thou wilt have a tale to tell, which will help the hours to pass merrily. Hast thou any tidings? Is there any fresh news from the Holy Land?"

"Little of importance," replied the supposed palmer. "But before I tell my story, perhaps thou wilt answer me a few inquiries, for I confess I am mightily curious about this same hall of thine. I had thought this was the hall of Staley."

"And so it is, Sir Palmer. What belike should make thee doubt it?"

"Well, friend, I have travelled in the Holy Land myself, and thy master's escutcheon is not unknown to me. He was a stout soldier of King Richard against the Paynim. And that banner which floats from the high tower bears not the same devise as that which Sir Ro of Staley bravely upheld against the Saracens."

"In truth, thou art right there, Sir Palmer. 'Tis not the same banner, and, though I eat my salt beneath the new devise, I do not mind confessing that I would sooner see the old one flying overhead. 'Tis a sad story, friend. Hast thou not heard in thy wanderings that the brave knight of Staley was slain in the Holy Land?"

"That is news to me," answered the other, starting. "But even so, what of his lady? Is she not alive?"

The warder looked uneasily about him, as though he had no wish to talk upon such a subject.

"The women can tell thee more of my lady," said he. "And thou art still hungry. Eat first, and talk afterwards."

DOORWAY TO STALEY CHAPEL,
MOTTRAM CHURCH

Saying which he ushered Sir Ro to an apartment, and left him for a while to the attention of the waiting maids. As the warder, even so the maids—none recognised their lord, Sir Ro, in the palmer's garb which he was wearing. In accordance with the old laws of English hospitality, they brought to him a cup of methyglin, and manchets of bread to eat. As he supped, Sir Ro fell into conversation with the maids; he asked after the health of the Lady of Staley, and whether he might have an audience with her. To which the maids made answer that the Lady of Staley was sore troubled, and even then was weeping in her chamber, and would see no man. Then they related to him the circumstances of their lady's trouble. The knight of Staley, they said, had gone away to fight in the great crusade. News had come that he was dead—having been captured and put to death by the enemy—and now the kinsmen of the lady were forcing her to wed again, although her heart was still with her dead lord, and she could bear the sight of no other man.

"That," said the spokeswoman, "is why Staley Hall is so much changed, and why another banner floats above the turrets."

38

"But if your lady does not love the newcomer, why then does she submit to a marriage which must be distasteful? Did not her lord will his estates to her in case he should fall in the Crusade?"

"That we know not, good sir palmer. But 'tis said that this new knight has made her understand that he hath a grant of her late husband's lands from the king, and that he will dispossess both her and her relations unless she consents to marry him. Folk do think it is more for the sake of her kinsfolk that she brings her mind to the wedding."

"And when is the wedding to be?"

"To-morrow."

Sir Ro pondered awhile, then turning to the chief serving-maid, asked:

"Would'st do thy lady a service?"

Being answered in the affirmative, he took his empty drinking-cup, and dropped into it the half of his wife's broken wedding ring, which he had retained, and bade the maid carry it to her mistress. This the maid did. On seeing it, the Lady of Staley gave a great cry, and, saying that the palmer surely brought some news of her dead husband's last hours, and perchance carried his dying message, she commanded him to be brought into her presence.

Sir Ro now beheld the face of his loved one, whom he had never thought to see again. At first the lady failed to recognise in the guise of the palmer, the husband whom she had never ceased to love, and Sir Ro, being anxious to learn whether she was still true to him, forebore to make himself known. The lady, with tears in her eyes, looked at the half of the wedding ring which the palmer had brought, and placing her hand in her bosom drew forth the companion half which she wore ever near her heart. Then, with many sobs, she protested that the image of her dead lord had never left her, and that she only consented to mate with another in order that her kinsfolk should not be reduced to beggary.

Bit by bit the knight drew from her all the story: how her new suitor had been the one to bring tidings of her lord's death, and how he, having secured the Staley estates, now offered her the choice of a union with him or beggary for herself and her people.

Then Sir Ro, unable to restrain himself any longer, uttered her name in his own voice, and instantly she recognised him, and, with a great cry, fell into his arms.

EFFIGY OF SIR RO AND HIS LADY, IN STALEY CHAPEL, MOTTRAM CHURCH

Now the joyful cry uttered by the Lady of Staley rang throughout the hall, and, full of wonder and fear, the retainers rushed to the chamber, feeling that they had been indiscreet to leave her alone with an unknown palmer. The treacherous knight, who, by his lying tale, sought to entrap her into marriage, also appeared upon the scene, and, in a voice of anger, demanded of the palmer what he wanted, and by what right he was there.

"By the best right in the world," answered Sir Ro—"the right of master."

"Insolent," cried the traitor-knight in a fury, drawing his sword as he spake. "Thou shalt pay dearly for thy folly."

But Sir Ro, with a sharp action, cast from his shoulders the palmer's disguise, and, standing forth in the full glory of his warlike figure, snatched a mace from the wall, and advanced to meet his enemy.

"A Staley, a Staley!" he cried, giving forth the rallying cry of his house in a voice which the retainers knew of old.

Instantly he was recognised, and with shouts of joy the men-at-arms and servitors sprang to his side, whilst some of them disarmed the traitor, and without waiting for the order from their lord, hurried him to the deepest dungeon, there to await justice when the joyful celebrations anent Sir Ro's return had come to an end.

Needless to say the imposter met with the punishment he deserved; he was stripped of his knightly rank, and was never afterwards seen or heard of in Longdendale. The bells of Mottram Church rang out a merry peal in honour of the homecoming of the Knight of Staley. Sir Ro and his lady lived a long and happy life together. At their death they were buried in Mottram Church, where an effigy was placed to their memory above their grave. This effigy, which represents a knight in full armour, and his lady lying side by side, may still be seen in the Staley Chapel of the old Church at Mottram, and it serves to keep green the story of Sir Ro's adventures.

Author's Note

In Mottram Church is an ancient monumental effigy, which is said to represent the figures of Sir Ro or Ralph de Stavelegh of Staley Hall and his wife—the hero and heroine of the foregoing legend. "Roe Cross," the name of a well-known spot in Mottram, is also attributed to the connection of the place with this popular local crusader.

VI

Robin Hood's Visit to Longdendale

ROBIN HOOD, the greatest bowman that old England ever knew, frequently visited Longdendale. Probably the "thick woods of Longden," with their wealth of wild red deer, induced him to lead his band from the haunts of merrie Sherwood to the no less merrie land of Longdendale. Old traditions tell of a "mighty forest in Longdendale, whose trees were so thick that the squirrels could leap from branch to branch from Mottram to Woodhead." Such a country might well attract a lover of the free forest life like bold Robin Hood; moreover, there ran a road over a good portion of Longdendale, along which the fat old Abbots of Basingwerke were wont to convey their treasures from their township of Glossop, to their fine abbey seat in Wales. Doubtless the Abbot dreaded a meeting with the mighty outlaw, for Robin dearly loved to pluck a fat-bellied churchman that he might place the golden nobles in the pouches of the poor.

This story, however, has nothing to do with the robbing of the Abbots or Monks of Basingwerke. It is a story of skill and fabulous strength. Indeed, there are many who doubt that the incidents related ever occurred—simply because such things seem impossible. But then those incidents are recorded in the traditions of the people of Longdendale, and, consequently, they are worthy of serious consideration. He must be either an amazingly bold or an exceedingly ignorant man, who would cast a doubt on the veracity of a Longdendale tradition.

However, the reader must judge for himself.

The story has it that bold Robin Hood and his forest band (including the redoubtable Little John, Friar Tuck, Will Scarlet, and Much, the miller's son, and a hundred other sturdy yeomen, all clad in Lincoln green, and having great long bows of English yew and good cloth-yard shafts) appeared one day in the Longdendale country. Weary of hunting the stag through the woodland glades, they were longing for some chance of adventure to present itself, when they became aware of a loud and dismal moaning hard by. The sound came from a handsome youth who, cast full length upon the sward, was bitterly bemoaning his cruel fate. It appeared that he was betrothed to a beautiful maiden, but her guardian (who was a grim old bachelor) had forbidden their union, and finally, to prevent all intercourse between them, had shut her up in his castle.

On hearing the story the foresters were loud in their denunciations of such heartless conduct. They vowed it was the greatest sin that man could possibly commit—to interfere with lover's meetings. Little John was for attacking the castle, battering down the gates, and sending an arrow through the mid-rib of the guardian, which process, he thought, was calculated to end the matter at once. But Robin, though anxious enough for a fight, was of opinion that his henchman's plan might endanger the maiden, who was completely at the mercy of the tyrant. He suggested an interview, and, accordingly, the stout Friar Tuck was sent as ambassador or emissary to make terms with the maiden's guardian.

At first the Friar was met with an angry outburst on the part of the guardian—a bold bad baron—who loudly declaimed that he would permit no outside interference with his affairs.

"Out on thee, thou fat-bellied churchman," shouted the Baron. "What hast thou to do with lovers, particularly maidens. Methinks thy vows should bid thee leave maids and love severely alone."

Now this sort of talk did not at all suit Friar Tuck, who, churchman though he might be, and shaven and shorn to boot, yet loved to kiss a pretty maid on the sly as well as the best layman who ever walked. But he loved not to be twitted about it in this fashion.

"Fat-bellied churchman, indeed," quoth he. "And what about thine own fat paunch. As for love and pretty maids, I warrant thou would'st have a long way to travel fore thou comest across a maiden who would fall in love with thee. Such a foul-visaged reptile I never set eyes on. As for beauty—well, as far as thou art concerned—the least said on that head the better."

The Baron stared at this rejoinder, as well he might. Such language had never been hurled at him before, and for a moment

43

he could scarcely speak, so great was his surprise. When he recovered speech, he ordered his attendants who were in the room to seize the Friar and cast him into the dungeon. But Tuck lifted the quarter-staff which he carried, and brought it down so heavily upon their crowns that the men dropped like poled oxen. At this the Baron began to swear and rave, vowing all manner of punishments for the Friar,—all of which, however, only made Tuck fall a-laughing.

"Come," said he, "thou art short of wind enough, friend Baron. And if thou goest on like that thou art like to choke thyself. Moreover, if thou only so much as raises a finger to summon thy vassals to thy side with intent to lay me by the heels, I shall een clout thee on the sconce as I have served thy catiffs. So thou hadst best listen to reason."

Now sorely discomfited as he was, a bright idea suddenly struck the Baron, and turning blandly to the Friar, he readily consented to set free the maiden, and to permit her marriage with her handsome lover, providing the foresters (of whose shooting prowess he had heard so much) could shoot their arrows from the tumulii now called "The Butts" to the upright Druid stones, now known by the name of "Robin Hood's Picking Rods." By setting them this (apparently impossible) task, he thought to rid himself of interference from the band; and he chuckled merrily to himself, when Tuck (who knew nothing of the distance to be covered by the archers) coolly accepted the terms.

The time for the shooting display having arrived, the Baron led a gay company to the scene, that he and all his friends might witness the discomfiture of the renowned archers of Sherwood. As for the handsome youth on whose behalf Robin had interfered, he was quite dismayed, and even the assurance of the outlaw could not comfort him, for he thought the feat impossible.

The archers stood at the butts, and away in the distance rose the stone target of "The Picking Rods." Robin Hood took the first shot, and he laughed inwardly as he drew the string tight and true. For he knew the secret of the "Long Bow"—(as, indeed, do the chroniclers who tell this story). The arrow left the bow with a shrill whistle of the goose-wing tip, and, greatly to the surprise of the

Baron, it fell plump on the target with such force as to cut a notch in the hard stone,—a notch so deep that it may be seen to this day. Little John, Will Scarlet, and the rest of the forest band, all tried their skill, and but few failed to hit the mark, though none were quite so near the centre as their leader Robin Hood.

When the shooting was finished the Baron was in a great rage, and he sought for some means of evading the fulfilment of his promise. Turning to Robin Hood he made an offer—that if the outlaw, with his own hands, cast down the great stone which stood upon Werneth Low, then the Baron would not only bestow the maiden upon her lover, but would give her a good dowry into the bargain. On the other hand, if Robin failed to accomplish the task, the whole matter must rest where it was, and the maiden remain a captive.

Greatly to the surprise of all, Robin agreed to the proposal.

"I will humour thee this once," said he to the Baron. "But if thou attemptest to get behind thy word when the feat is done, my good foresters shall fall upon thee and knock sparks out of thy baronial hide."

"If thou doest the feat," quoth the Baron, "rest assured I shall keep my promise."

For the task he had set bold Robin was, as the Baron well knew, a thousand times more difficult than that of shooting at the Picking Rods.

Robin Hood conversed awhile with Friar Tuck, and then the whole company moved off to the summit of Werneth Low. The stone, or rock, as it should more properly be called, was a huge mass almost the height of a man. It had occupied its position on the summit of Werneth since the world was created. A round half-dozen of the Baron's retainers failed to lift it. But Robin Hood, casting aside his jerkin, and baring his brawny arm, raised the great stone slowly aloft, and then, with one mighty throw, cast it out westward towards the sunset, and, amid a wild shout of triumph, it disappeared in the distance.

They afterwards found the stone in the bed of the River Tame, near the woods of Arden, and, under the name of "Robin Hood's Stone" it remains in that same spot to this day.

"THE ROBIN HOOD STONE"

Now there are some who profess to believe that no mortal power could cast that stone so great a distance, and they explain the event by supposing that Robin was in league with the good fairies, who gave him strength to lift the stone, and then, (invisible to men) flew away with it, and dropped it in the Tame. And perhaps these people may be right.

Be that as it may, there is no record to show that the bold bad Baron disbelieved in Robin's powers, and we may take it for granted that the lovely maiden was duly released, that she married the lad of her choice, and that they lived happy ever afterwards, as they certainly deserved to do.

It is asserted by some that there was a much smaller stone near the great Robin Hood Stone on Werneth Low, and that Little John afterwards threw this stone in the direction of the one thrown by Robin. The second stone, being lighter, travelled a few yards further than the first, but the throw being not so skilful the stone was broken in several pieces by the fall. It lies to this day near the

Robin Hood Stone in the waters of the River Tame, and it still retains the name of that giant forester Little John.

Author's Note

The "Robin Hood relics," referred to in the foregoing legend, are objects of great local interest and curiosity. The "Robin Hood's Picking Rods" are situated on Ludworth Moor, and consist of portions of two upright stone pillars rising from a massive stone base. They are thought by many to be relics of the Druidical period, and are referred to in the "Legend of Coombs Rocks"—the first legend of the present series. It is said that they received their present name because Robin Hood and his outlaws used them as a target for their arrows, and the dents in the pillars are said to have been caused by the arrow points.

The "Robin Hood Stone" is a huge rock which lies in the bed of the River Tame near the Denton Cemetery at Hulme's Wood, almost opposite the Arden Paper Mill.

As stated in the legend, there are fragments of Little John's stone near it, and old traditions state that both stones were thrown to their present positions from the top of Werneth Low by the two foresters whose names they bear. Certain indentations in the larger stone are said to be the imprints of the fingers of Robin Hood, whose grip was so strong that he left the impression in the solid stone.

VII

The Abbot of Basingwerke

Or The Wehr-Wolf of Longdendale

GLOSSOP, which in the Doomsday survey was reckoned as part of Longdendale, was granted by William the Conqueror to his natural son, William Peveril—Peveril of the Peak,—whose descendant was disinherited by Henry II. for procuring the death of the Earl of Chester by poison, when the township reverted to the Crown. King Henry, however, being on a military expedition to North Wales, became acquainted with the monks of Basingwerke, and in return for their friendship and attention he bestowed the township upon Basingwerke Abbey.

A road which crosses a portion of Longdendale is known as The Monk's Road, and is so called because the Monks of Basingwerke are said to have made and used it. On the wildest part of this road stands a large stone, hollowed out in the shape of a rude seat, which is said to have been the seat of the Abbot of Basingwerke, who periodically held open-air court on that spot. The stone is known as "The Abbot's Chair."

On a certain day in the reign of good King Henry, the Abbot of Basingwerke sat in state upon the stone seat of "The Abbot's Chair." He was holding a court for the receipt of all his rents and tithes, for the dispensation of justice in that part of his possessions, and for the purpose of hearing any petitions which the people might wish to make. To him came an old dame, full of woe and misery, and almost blind with the falling of bitter tears. Her tale was enough to melt the stoutest heart. She had an enemy, and the enemy was a woman who dabbled in witchcraft. Through the agency of evil spirits, this witch had brought death upon the old dame's husband and on all her children, so that now she was all alone in the world, and knew not where to look for shelter or for bread. It was said, also, that the witch possessed the power of

48

changing her shape, appearing now as a woman, now as a man, now as an animal or bird, so that it was almost impossible to catch her and bring her for punishment.

The Abbot of Basingwerke, on hearing the story, was very angry. He first relieved the distress of the poor woman, and then pronounced an awful curse upon the wicked witch.

"May the hand of Heaven fall upon this wicked mortal," cried the Abbot, "and in whatever shape she be at the present moment, may that shape cling to her until justice has been done."

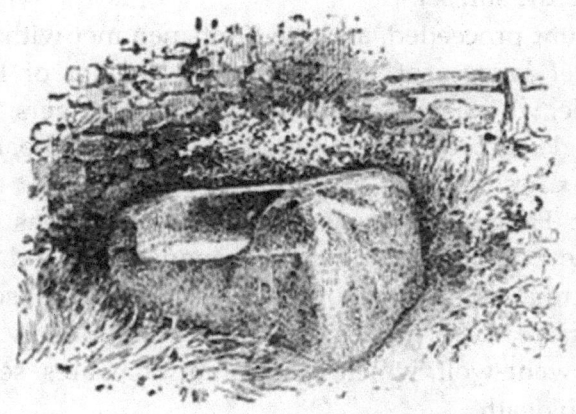

"THE ABBOT'S CHAIR"

Then he prophesied that ere long the righteous wrath of heaven would fall upon the witch, and that a bitter death would assuredly be her portion. And the old dame went away satisfied.

Now it chanced that that very morning the witch had changed herself into a wehr-wolf, and was even then prowling about the forest in search of victims. And by further good luck it happened that good King Henry II., who was on a visit to the Baron of Ashton-under-Lyne, was out hunting in company with his son, Prince Henry, the Lord of Longdendale, the Baron of Ashton, and other noblemen and knights of the district, The Royal party hunted chiefly in the forests of Longdendale, which were noted for wild boars, deer, and game of every description. And inasmuch as it was customary at a Royal hunt for every portion of the forest to be explored, and all the game therein, great and small, driven forth before the hunters, there was—providing there was any efficacy in the Abbot's curse—every prospect of the wicked old witch being immediately laid by the heels. On former occasions when she had assumed the form of an animal, it had always been easy for her, if pursued, to fly into the nearest thicket, and there resume her human shape, or else to suddenly disappear altogether. But if the Abbot's curse took effect and compelled her to remain in the garb of a wehr-wolf, then it was almost certain that she would meet her doom before the sun set.

The hunt proceeded, and the huntsmen met with good sport, but the chief success of the day fell to the lot of the Lord of Longdendale, who slew "several horrible British tigers," and after a tough struggle succeeded in killing the largest wild boar which was ever seen in Cheshire.

Prince Henry, who was a valiant youth, was desirous of imitating the exploits of the Lord of Longdendale, and accordingly he repaired to a gloomy part of the forest in search of some worthy adventure. Here, to his great surprise, he was suddenly set upon by a fierce old wehr-wolf, which, taking him unawares, seemed likely to put him to death.

BASE OF CROSS ON THE MONKS' ROAD

At the first assault the Prince's steed, by swerving as the

wehr-wolf sprang, luckily saved the rider, and Prince Henry was enabled to bring his hunting spear to bear upon the beast. He drove at it, and although he succeeded in piercing its side, so that it cried out horribly—more like a human cry than a beast's, said the Prince, when he afterwards came to recount the story of the combat—yet it seized the spear handle in its forepaws, and with a snap of its great jaws broke the spear clean in two, so that the Royal huntsman was left almost defenceless. He drew out his long hunting-knife and buried it to the hilt as the beast sprang at him, but though he fought bravely and long, the terrible thing succeeded in pulling him from his horse to the ground. Here the Prince gripped the beast by the throat, but his strength was much spent, and it seemed almost certain that he must succumb. Fortunately, however, he had been followed at a distance by the Baron of Ashton, who arrived upon the spot just in time to turn the fight, and to engage and finally slay the wehr-wolf.

Great honour was, of course, bestowed upon the Baron of Ashton, and the carcase of the wolf was taken in triumph to the Castle at Ashton-under-Lyne. Upon the beast being opened, its stomach was found to contain the heads of three babes which it had devoured that morning.

Much talk then ensued as to the unusual fierceness shown by the wehr-wolf, and the Prince again and again asserted that at times the cries of the beast were most human in sound. A forester, also, on hearing of the exploit, came forward and gave some strange testimony.

"May it please your highness," said he, "I was to-day lying in a doze beneath the greenwood, whither I had crawled to hide, the better to enable me to watch and ambush certain forest marauders who interfere with the deer, when I was suddenly startled by a strange noise, and, on looking through the copse, beheld a wehr-wolf tearing at its own skin as though it desired to cast it off, even as a man discards his clothes. And the thing screamed and moaned piteously, and it seemed to me that a woman's cracked voice, muttering wild incantations, emerged from the beast's throat. Upon hearing which I was sore afraid, thinking I was bewitched by the evil one, and I fled."

51

Divers others had also strange tales to tell of the wehr-wolf's actions, and that same evening, on the Abbot of Basingwerke coming to dine with the Royal hunting party at the hall of Ashton-under-Lyne, it was proved beyond doubt that the wehr-wolf was none other than the wicked witch.

Thus was the curse of the Abbot speedily fulfilled and justice meted out. Needless to say that witch was never seen again.

VIII

The Devil's Elbow

THE traveller through the valley of the Etherow is invariably impressed with the wild grandeur of the scenery, and in nine cases out of ten his attention is especially claimed by the bold rock escarpment known as "The Devil's Elbow," which frowns high over the course of the stream. The situation of the rock is certainly romantic: the wild moorlands of bog and heather stretch away on either side, in fact the rock stands on the verge of some of the wildest mountain scenery of Great Britain. The very name of the place is suggestive of legend, and one is not surprised to learn that there are some queer stories related concerning the neighbourhood; one of these explains how the rock came to receive its name.

The date of the story is uncertain—that fact, however, should not trouble the reader. At the time when the events now to be related actually occurred, there was a castle standing on one of the heights above the Etherow; it was a strong castle, fit home for a proud old feudal lord; and its owner, De Morland, was one of the most haughty of those barons who claimed descent from the great Norman lords who landed with William the Conqueror. Little is known of him beyond the fact that he was immensely proud of his long ancestry, that he was very fierce, that he was rich, and looked with scorn upon most of the gentry of the neighbourhood. These things certainly do not speak much for his good sense, for why a man should imagine that the possession of a few more pieces of gold or silver makes him a better man than his neighbour, is a mystery. For instance, a thief may by successful robbery become wealthier than an honest poor man, but surely the mere possession of greater wealth does not make him better than the poor man. The principle of this holds good with regard to wealth, no matter how it may have been secured. So, after all, the Baron de Morland had no sound base on which to build up his pride.

The baron had a daughter named Geraldine, who was born on May day, and was as sweet as the month in which she was born.

53

Her teeth were like pearls, her hair gleamed like gold, her skin was the fairest, and her figure the most beautiful ever known in Longdendale. Altogether she was a maid to set the hearts of men aflame with love.

Now it should be stated at the outset that the maiden had been wooed by more than one noble suitor, but she had an eye to none save a brave young knight who came from Mottram. His name was Sir Mottram de Mossland, and he was lord of a castle—something similar in appearance to that of the Baron de Morland, but not quite so grand—which stood on a bold ridge near Mottram town. This knight had long been in love with the lady Geraldine, and on several occasions had managed to get interviews with his lady-love. We may be sure he lost no time in making known to her the state of his heart, and in ascertaining the exact condition of her own. They kissed, and swore fidelity to each other, and generally behaved like all young lovers do. But bye and bye the Baron de Morland got to hear of this lover's business, and he swore a terrible oath concerning it.

"THE LADY GERALDINE"

"By my halidome," swore he, in the hearing of his daughter; "Who is this upstart de Mossland? Are his lands to be compared with mine? Is his name to be linked with that of de Morland? Shall one of his hated blood mate with my own superior stock. Out upon the thought. I will slay him sooner. Yea, by my halidome, and all the saints whom I adore, I swear most solemnly that if I know him to speak another word with my daughter, it shall be the last word he shall ever speak. For I will have his blood."

The Lady Geraldine heard this terrible oath, and knowing the character of her furious parent well, was quite certain that he would carry out his threat. So, fearing for the

54

safety of her lover, she had a message conveyed to him, begging him, if he really cared for her, to cease his stolen visits for a time. The lover, though sorely troubled, obeyed her requests, and the days passed by in fruitless sighing and longing.

Of course, it goes without saying, that, although he might refrain from speaking to the maid, a handsome and brave gallant like Sir Mottram de Mossland would yet be on the alert to secure a glimpse of his lady-love, and would worship her with his eyes even if his lips were doomed to be closed. And so it came to pass that, day by day, often in disguise, he followed her path, and gazed longingly at her from a distance. Now, one day when she was out riding on her milk-white palfrey, her steed took fright, and ran away, and would certainly have leaped down a dreadful precipice—carrying the lady to death,—if the gallant Sir Mottram had not sprung at its head, and pulled it, by main force, to a place of safety.

Now, in spite of his lady-love's message, he could no longer refrain from speaking, and, folding her in his arms, he kissed her, and asked for some token of love in return. The maid kissed him gladly, and promised to marry him in spite of her stern and cruel father. Then, full of joy, Sir Mottram went on his way singing gaily, for his heart was lifted up by the promise of his lady-love.

Unfortunately, however, the Baron de Morland was riding that way, and when he beheld the transports of Sir Mottram he immediately guessed what had been toward, and he at once began to swear again. No oath was too strong for him to use concerning the family of Sir Mottram de Mossland. It should be stated in explanation, that years before, the Baron had been in love with Sir Mottram's mother—then a pretty maiden in her teens—and had been rejected by her in favour of Sir Mottram's father. Hence the Baron de Morland could never bear the sight or mention of a de Mossland, and hence his hatred of a union between Sir Mottram and his daughter Geraldine.

Full of anger the Baron rode home to his castle, and there at once sent for his daughter.

"You minx," cried he, "is't true that you have promised yourself to that foul de Mossland?"

"It is true, my father," said Geraldine, in a low yet clear voice. "What else could I do since I love him? Moreover, he is not a foul knight, but is brave and true."

Now the Baron swore again.

"You witch," he cried, "know this, rather than you should wed de Mossland—yea, by all the saints I swear it!—I will send you to the devil."

"Oh, my father!" shrieked Geraldine, "have mercy!"

And her shrieks rang through the castle, till the serving maids and the men-at-arms came running in to see what was the matter.

But the Baron took up his sword, and with the flat of it struck right and left, and drove them forth. Then, turning once more to her, he shouted:

"Mark well what I say. If you speak to de Mossland again I will summon the devil's aid, and you shall be sorely punished."

Then he left the room, and the lady fainted.

Now, the Lady Geraldine was bold enough, as became a daughter born of a race of fighting men, and, having pledged her word to her lover, she had no intention of going from it. So, on the day appointed, she proceeded to a certain spot, where her lover met her, all prepared for flight. The lovers kissed, and then the knight began:

"Dear Geraldine," said he.—But before he could proceed further, an awful thing happened. A dark form rose up between them, and, on looking at it they knew it was the Devil. He was in his own shape, with horns, hoofs, and tail complete. With a mocking laugh he bent his elbow, and made as though to seize the maid, but Sir Mottram, throwing his arms about her, turned and fled, hoping to be able to cross a running stream before the devil could touch them, and then, by the laws of sorcery, they would be free from satanic molestation.

The devil, however, gained on them rapidly, and it appeared certain that he would catch them, when, just as he put out his hand to touch the maid, a strange light appeared in the sky, and a voice called out the one word—"Hold."

The Devil staggered as though he had been shot, and when he

recovered the light had vanished, and with it the maiden and her lover.

They were never seen again, but the legends say that they were made perfectly happy by the fairies, and that they still haunt the banks of the Etherow at certain seasons of the year in the forms of two white swans.

As for the devil, he received a shock. At the moment the light appeared, his right arm had been bent at the elbow for the purpose of seizing hold of his prey, but lo! when his victims had disappeared, he found that the powers which had delivered them from him had turned his right arm into stone. Not a muscle of it could he move, it would not bend, it was worse than useless, it was an encumbrance.

So Satan, being a philosopher in his way, determined to make the best of a bad job. He tore the arm out by the roots, and left it there—the elbow showing prominently over Longdendale. And that is how the great rock known as the Devil's Elbow came to be perched high up above the Etherow valley.

Author's Note

The Devil's Elbow is the name given to a picturesque rock which stands on the brow of a high and steep hill above the valley of the Etherow. This rock is one of the landmarks of the Longdendale country.

IX

The Legend of Charlesworth Chapel

AN old chapel at Charlesworth is said to have owed its foundation to the circumstances narrated in the following tradition.

Once upon a time—it is impossible to say exactly when, because, unfortunately, the records as to date have been lost, but it was certainly in that halcyon period of English history which is generally spoken of as "the olden time"—a traveller was on his way from the northern parts of England to London. Here again the chronicles are slightly obscure, because there is no mention of his name, and opinions differ as to his occupation. Some state that he was an Irish merchant, others that he was a priest. But be that as it may, all agree that he made the journey, that he made it on foot and alone. For the purposes of this story, therefore, it will suffice to refer to him as "The Traveller."

He had reached that portion of Derbyshire known as the Peak, and was journeying over that part of the Peak which includes Coombs Rocks and the hills above the River Etherow, when he found himself overtaken by the night-fall. The track he was travelling was but ill-defined; it led through a desolate region—in fact, one of the wildest regions in all Britain—and, therefore, was but seldom used. As a consequence it was no easy task to keep to it in broad daylight, and when the darkness enveloped the moor, the danger of losing it was very great. To-day, when almost every acre of the country is cultivated and drained, the neighbourhood though savage enough is comparatively a safe one to travel, but in the time of which we speak there were treacherous bogs on every side in which the unwary might easily be swallowed up.

Accustomed as he was to the perils and vicissitudes of a wandering life, the Traveller was, nevertheless, somewhat dismayed to find himself be-nighted so far from any habitation, and in a country altogether strange to him.

"Now may the good saints protect me," mused he, "for of a truth I am like to need their intercession this night. Already the

58

path grows fainter, the skies seem charged with rain, and the wind moans eerily."

He wrapped his cloak tighter about his limbs, and stepped along at a brisker pace.

"If only the night would clear," he said, "so that I could see distant objects, then should I be likely to make my way in safety from this desolate moor. But the darkness hangs heavy like a pall: it is damp as though the clouds were settling on the heather, and — ha!"

The last exclamation was wrung from him by the slipping of his foot, and the fact that he suddenly found himself standing up to the knees in the sponge-like peat. He turned his face and tried to retrace his steps, hoping to regain the path, but this was no easy task, and presently he found that he was wandering hopelessly through the bog, with every risk of becoming engulfed if he proceeded further. To make matters worse, at that moment, a thick white choking mist settled down on the moor, and it seemed to the Traveller that his fate was indeed sealed. He stretched out his staff in despair, and by great good luck it struck on firm grit, and in another moment the Traveller had hauled himself upon solid earth. Once here, prudence told him not to stir, either to the right hand or the left, lest all the horrors from which he had just escaped should be again about him. There was nothing for it but to wait patiently for the return of day, when he might be able to thread his way through the mazy bogs in safety. But the night was chill, the mist was like the icy touch of death, and in a little while the Traveller was shaking in every joint. The keen cold went to the bone, and it seemed as though he must now perish from exposure.

"Now indeed am I in a sorry plight," quoth he, "and I have need of the Divine help; else I am lost."

Whereupon, being a good Christian, he fell upon his knees, and prayed aloud to God for help, vowing that if he was permitted to reach his home again he would return to those hills, and as a thankoffering erect thereon a house of prayer dedicated to his patron saint.

Scarcely was the prayer ended when a great wind arose, the mists were rolled away like a curtain, the hill tops stood out in the clear night, the stars shone, and the moon-beams fell softly over the landscape, and a shepherd came along as though a heaven-sent guide to show him the path from the hills.

"Friend," said the shepherd simply, as he beheld the Traveller, "Hast thou been long upon the moor? If so, thou shouldst indeed be thankful to God, for thou hast run a great risk of losing thy life upon this desolate wilderness of heather."

"Thou sayest truly," replied the Traveller, who then proceeded to recount his experiences and his vow, and also asked the name of the place where they stood. Then he marked the spot, which lay upon the bleak hill-side above the present village of Charlesworth.

"I will surely come here again," said he, "if my life is spared, and fulfil my vow."

On concluding his journey, and having discharged his business, he immediately returned to the Peak, and on the spot of his delivery he built a small chapel or oratory of bog oak, which was specially brought over from Ireland. This building, says tradition, was erected upon the site now occupied by the present Charlesworth Chapel.

Why Irish bog oak should have been the material used in building, the present writer has not been able to discover, nor does the tradition in this particular altogether agree with the following account of what is therein stated to have been the original fabric.

"It was a small octagon chapel," says the historian, "the roof of which was carved; the arched rafters resting on massive buttresses, the walls rough blocks of stone, the floor earth covered with rushes, the seats and altar simple and unpretentious."

Possibly the building mentioned in this account was a successor of an even earlier structure, and to judge from other sacred buildings in the neighbourhood, it is by no means unlikely that the earliest chapel of all was one mainly composed of timber. But after all, what does it really matter whether the chapel was built of wood or stone, so long as the Traveller fulfilled his vow, and so long as the chapel served the purpose for which it was erected?

X

Sir Edmund Shaa

IN the reign of King Henry VI. there dwelt in Longdendale a youth who bore the name of Edmund Shaa. It is claimed by some that he was a native of Longdendale, but other authorities assert that he was born in the parish of Stockport. Certain it is that he was connected with the parish of Stockport, and also with that of Mottram—a connection which he maintained up to the close of his life. Moreover, the Shaas were among the earliest of the inhabitants of Mottram of whom we have reliable record, and the name Shaa, in its modernised form of Shaw, is still found in the town, and other portions of the parish.

At the period of our story, the Shaas were recognised as a family of great respectability, though not of much wealth. They probably belonged to the yeoman class, and for generations had been accustomed to live on the soil, passing their lives in the open air, varying the hours of toil with the healthy recreations then common—shooting with the bow, sword-play, or indulging in the chase. Healthy, manly lives they led, fearing God, obeying the laws, and paying their way honestly enough, with a margin left over to provide against a rainy day—but by no means able to amass any great store of wealth. Besides Edmund Shaa, his father, John Shaa, had other sons, of whom, however, little is known.

The boyhood of Edmund Shaa passed like that of other Longdendale children, exhibiting no signs of extraordinary promise, unless the bright alertness and the ambitious imaginings of the lad might be accounted as such. But as he grew older, there came over the boy an unconquerable aversion to the unchanging life of the country. Not that the life itself was disagreeable, but the labour seemed all in vain, never leading to anything better than the humble respectability which was the highest mark of yeoman rank. Young Edmund Shaa had seen the trains of noble knights pass by; he had witnessed the huntings in the forests of Longdendale, when lords and ladies gay rode in grand attire, on richly-caparisoned steeds, and received every mark of respect from the country people who assembled to witness the sport. And to his young brain, it seemed that the best of them all was but a mortal of flesh and blood and intelligence, like any yeoman's son and daughter, or even as the hinds. Was not he, Edmund Shaa, as well made, as shapely, as strong, as keen of intellect as any of the rich gallants who flaunted themselves in silken attire before his eyes; and that being so, why should not he, putting his abilities to use, come to attain a position of power and affluence equal to theirs?

The young lad thought the matter out many a time, and to him there seemed but one reason—the lack of opportunity. In Longdendale he had no chance of distinguishing himself. There was no wealth to be won in Longdendale,—nay, even the very abilities which he knew himself to possess were not recognised by his fellows—for is it not a worldwide truism that "a prophet is not without honour save in his own country?"

Then the lad decided in his own mind that he must leave his Cheshire home, and seek occupation elsewhere, if he was to become anything better than a yeoman. He accordingly sought counsel of his elders—his relatives and friends—and made known his ambitions to them. But the elders only laughed at him, and discouraged his scheming.

"Banish all such dreams from thy foolish pate," said one. "Thou art a good lad, and a clever one to boot, but the life thy fathers led is good enough for thee. Lords and ladies are above thy station; thou wilt have to work for thy living, and, as for holding thy head high, and bothering thy brains with affairs of State—why, lad, thou art a fool to think about it."

Such discouragement was kindly meant, but other folk, to whom the lad told his hopes and longings, were less sympathetic. Some openly jeered at him, called him a dreamer, denounced him as a conceited fop, upbraided him with the fault of considering himself superior to other people, and finally snubbed him and treated him as a snob.

Young Shaa bore all this quietly enough in the presence of his tormentors; but the bitterness of it was keenly felt by him, and when alone, he gave way to grief. Often he would seek the quiet of some secluded spot in the woodland glades of Longdendale, and sob as though his heart would break, for it seemed that the obstacles in his path were too great for him to overcome.

One day when he thus lay lamenting in solitude over his fate, a great weariness stole over him, the hot summer's day overpowered him, and presently he fell into a doze. Then it was that the good fairies stole from their tiny palaces under the leaves in the forest, where no mortal may ever find them even if he looks, and, taking pity upon the handsome youth who lay sleeping near, decided to help him to achieve that goal of greatness upon which his soul was set. The little sprites gathered around him, and whispered in his ears a wondrous tale of the wealth and honour awaiting in London town all those bold English lads who dared seek fortune there. They drew phantom pictures of a young man's struggle in London, of his success by honest industry and skill, of civic functions in which the young man bore a part, of a grand procession, where the youth,—now grown to manhood's prime,— was become Lord Mayor; and to Edmund Shaa, who saw the pictures in his sleep, it seemed as though the face of that phantom Lord Mayor was his own face.

Then the fairies sang a song, and the words of the dream song were these:—

> "If thou would'st win great renown,
> Make thy way to London town;
> Fortune waits to greet thee there
> Even London's civic chair;
> Lord Mayor of London thou shalt be
> —The wielder of authority.
> And when thou rulest London town
> The King shall beg of thee his crown."

Shaa awoke with a start, sat up, and rubbed his eyes, telling himself that he had been dreaming—a wondrous pleasant dream,— but to his charmed ears there still came the sweet strains of the music, and the words of the fairy song:—

"If thou would'st win great renown,
Make thy way to London town.
London town, London town."

The lad listened awhile, then sprang to his feet with a joyful cry, and a determined look in his eyes.

"To London town," quoth he. "To London town! Thither I will go, and nought shall stop me now."

Then with a merry whistle, he made off homewards, and before the sun set, had completed his preparations for the long journey to the south.

The rest of Shaa's story reads like some romance, and yet it is true. Once settled in London, he appears to have been successful even beyond his wildest dreams. He became a member of the goldsmith's company, and rising rapidly in wealth and civic position, was ultimately appointed jeweller to King Edward IV.— and this position he continued to hold under four successive monarchs. In the year 1482 he received the dignity of Lord Mayor of London, and henceforth he became one of the most striking and interesting figures in that most dramatic period of English history. He received the honour of knighthood, and his influence was sufficiently powerful to render him one of the most prominent factors in securing the crown of England for King Richard III.

When Edward IV. died in 1483, it fell to the lot of Shaa, as Lord Mayor of London, to attend and take part in the funeral ceremonies, and to receive in great state the infant King Edward V., on his subsequent entry to the city. This occurred on May 4th, 1483, and is thus described in the old chronicle:—"When the Kynge approached nere the citie, Edmund Shaa, goldsmith, then Mayre, with William Whyte and John Matthewe, Sheriffs, and all the other Aldermene, in scarlette, with five hundred horse of the citizens in violette, received him reverentleye at Harnesey, and rydyng from thence accompanyed him into the city."

Richard, Duke of Gloucester, anxious to seize upon the crown, saw that the only way to accomplish his design was to secure the sympathies and support of the city of London. Being at that time Protector, he made Lord Mayor Shaa a member of the

Privy Council, and, after that, he seems to have had no difficulty in inducing him to enlist his sympathy and influence on the side of the plotters, and to secure the services of his brother,—Dr. Shaa—an Austin Friar, and a noted preacher of his day. The initial steps taken, the Shaas played conspicuous and important parts in the critical events which followed. Dr. Shaa preached at St. Paul's Cross against the legitimacy of Edward's children, and in advocacy of the claims of Richard; and Lord Mayor Shaa headed a deputation to Gloucester with an offer of the crown, and after the proclamation he attended as cup-bearer of the King. The citizens of London, however, began to suspect that the sons of their late King (Edward VI.) had been murdered, and showed signs of rebellion, upon which, Richard sent for over 5,000 soldiers to form his bodyguard, and not daring to levy money for the purpose of rewarding them, he disposed of some of the Crown property to Sir Edmund Shaa, who found means to supply the sum required. After the death of Richard at Bosworth Field, Shaa lived more the life of a private citizen, though he still continued to hold office as a magistrate and as the Royal Jeweller, and enjoyed the friendship and confidence of King Henry VII., until his death. During the latter portion of his career he had been associated with the most influential men of his time, honours had fallen thickly upon him, and his relations had become connected with families whose representatives are still to be found in the British Peerage, and among the older landed gentry.

It is pleasing to know that although Sir Edmund Shaa figured so prominently in great historic events of his day, he did not forget the northern county that gave him birth. He founded the old Grammar School at Stockport, and left a considerable sum of money with which to endow it. He gave a sum of money towards the cost of the building of the tower of Mottram Church. He also built a chapel in the Longdendale valley, at Woodhead, to which he thus refers in his will.

"I woll have two honest preestes, one of them to syng his mass and say his other divine service in a chapel that I have made in Longdendale, in the Countie of Chester; and to pray especially for my soule, and for the soules of my father and mother, and all Christian people; and I woll that he have for his salarie yerely for evermore, the sume of £4 6s. 8d.; and I woll that the other honest preeste be a discrete man, and coning in gramer."

The will of Sir Edmund Shaa is a curious yet beautiful specimen of the old English testamentary document. It begins thus—"In the name of God be it, Amen. The xxth day of the monthe of Marche, the yeare of our Lord after tha' compt of the Church of England mcccclxxxvijth, and iijth yeare of the reigne of Kinge Henry the vijth, I, Edmund Shaa, Knight Cytezen and Goldsmith and Alderman and Late Mayor of the Citie of London etc.... First I bequeathe and reccomend my soule to my Lord Jesus Christe, my Maker and my Redeemer; to the most glorious Virgin his mother, our Lady Saint Marye; to the full glorious Confessor, Saint Dunstan, and to the Holy Company of Heaven, and my body to be buryed in the Church of St Thomas of Acres in London, between the Pyler of the same Churche, whereupon the image of Sainte Mychel, the Archangel, standeth before the Auter, there called Saint Thomas Auter, and the nether ende of the same that is to wit as nigh the same as my body may reasonably be layed.... And in consideration that I have bourne the office of Mayoralte of the said City, I will for the honour of the same City, that my body be brought from my house to the Parish Church of St. Petery's, in Chepe, where I am a Parysshen as the Manor is, and from there to my burying at St. Thomas's, of Acres aforesaid, in descrete and honest wise without pomp of the world, and I will have xxiiij (24) honest torches to be bourne by xxiiij paide persons to convey my body from my house to my said Parisshe Churche as the maner is and so to my burying aforesaid, and I will have the same xxiiij torches and my honest tapers to be holden in like wise by iiij poor persons to brenne at my exequies to be doon for my soul as well at my burying aforesaid as at my Moneth's Mynde to be done for me. And I will that eache of the torch bearers and taper holders have for their suche labours to pray for my soule after all my said Exequyes full doon xxd."

The will then goes on to say—translated into modern English—"And, as the usage of the City of London, at the burial of one who hath borne the office of mayoralty is, for the mayor and aldermen, and other worshipful and honest commoners, to be present in their proper persons;—to the extent that they may understand that I was a true loving brother of theirs, and am in perfect charity with them, and each of them—if it would like the mayor and aldermen and recorder of the City of London, to be present at my Dirge and Mass of Requiem to be done for me; I would tenderly desire them, after the said Mass, to take such a repast as my executors by the sufferance of our Lord God, shall provide for them; and I will that each of them after his repast, have of my gift, from the hands of my executors, to remember my soul among their devout meditations, inasmuch as I am a brother of theirs, 6s. 8d." Among local bequests, the will contained the following—"I will that my executors, as soon as they may goodly after my decease, do buy so much Welsh frieze, half white, half black or gray, and thereof do make at my cost, 200 party gowns; and the 200 party gowns with 12d. in money along with every gown, I will be given to 200 poor persons dwelling in the parish of Stopford, in the County of Chester, whereat 'my fader and moder lyen buryed,' and within the parishes of Cheadle and Mottram in Longdendale in the said County, and in the parishes of Manchester, Ashton, Oldham, and Saddleworth, in the County of Lancaster, by the counsel and advice of the curates of the said parishes, ... such curates taking counsel with the saddest men dwelling in their parishes, to the intent that those poor persons should have them that have most need unto them." He also wills that his executors make at his cost "sixteen rings of fine gold, to be graven with the Well of Pity, the Well of Mercy, and the Well of Everlasting Life; with all other images and other things concerning the same—the rings to be distributed to certain persons named in the will." He also again refers to "the saide Church of Stopford" (Stockport) and the grave therein where the bodies of his father and mother "lyen buried."

Sir Edmund Shaa died on April 20th, 1487, just a month after making his will, and was buried according to his direction in "the Church of St. Thomas of Acres in London." He left behind him a widow—Dame Juliana, one son, Hugh, and two daughters, Katherine and Margaret. Hugh Shaa did not long survive his father, and died without male issue. It only remains to be added in conclusion that Shakespeare has immortalized Sir Edmund Shaa.

XI

Lord Lovel's Fate

THE Lovel family came into possession of the township of Mottram at an early period. In the time of Edward III. Sir John Lovel held the lordship of Longdendale from the King (as Earl of Chester) by military service. Sir John was a warrior of great bravery and fame. He served through the French wars, and in 1368 is mentioned as a leader under the Duke of Clarence. Most of the Lovels figure in history, and Francis, Lord Viscount Lovel, was a great favourite with Richard III. He was the King's chief Butler and Chamberlain of the Household. Moreover, he exercised a great influence in shaping the course of English affairs of his day. He was the Lovel of the ancient couplet:—

> The cat, the rat, and Lovel the dog,
> Rule all England under a hog.

The cat was Catesby, the rat Ratcliffe or Radcliffe, of Ordsall Hall, Salford, and the hog represented the crookbacked King.

Francis Lovel was looked upon by his tenants in Mottram as a being of almost equal importance to the King. His word was law, his favour was courted, his anger feared. There are many curious stories told concerning his connection with Mottram and its neighbourhood. It is said that he owned a hall in Mottram which was connected by a subterranean passage with the Parish Church. He is also the hero of many adventures, most of which may be set down as pure stories of imagination. Perhaps the following legend is of this class.

Now it should be stated that at the period of which we speak there were witches in Longdendale. The age was one of gross superstition, and it was universally believed that certain mortals, notably old women, were in league with the evil one, and that Satan had bestowed upon them powers of evil whereby they were enabled to work harm upon the persons of any to whom they took

68

a dislike. What particular powers these wretched women possessed will probably never be known; it is quite possible that some of them were students of magic, for in those ages some of the most learned men professed to dabble in mystic arts; but the probability is that by far the greater part of their dreaded powers existed only in the superstitious imaginings of the day. But to the people of that time the witches and their witchcraft were real enough and terrible to boot; so much so that if a man fell ill, or if some piece of bad luck befell him, to all the suffering caused thereby was added the mental torture consequent upon the belief that all the trouble had been caused by the evil schemes of some demon-possessed witch-woman. This belief was widespread, even among the better educated classes, to such an extent, that if a person lay ill of consumption, it was supposed that his waxen image was at that moment slowly melting before some witch-woman's fire, and that every fresh pang of pain was caused by the witch thrusting her sharp bodkin into the image. In Longdendale it was asserted that at night the witches sailed across the bleak moors seated on broomsticks. Often would the peasants rush in terror to the shelter of their cots as they heard a strange rustling overhead, and, on looking up, beheld the wizened forms of old hags riding on broomsticks through the air with a speed which no horse could equal.

There are certain stories told which ascribe to Lord Lovel the habit of consulting and using the services of these unholy mortals, but implicit faith cannot be placed upon these stories, because other tales describe him as absolutely fearless and devoid of superstition—a man, in fact, who placed no faith in their supposed powers.

On one occasion Lovel was in Longdendale. History does not tell us the cause of his visit, but he had left his hall at Mottram, and was walking in the woodland, when suddenly he found himself confronted by a woman of evil shape. She was an old hag, of bent form and wrinkled face, and she leaned heavily upon a crutch. For all that when she walked she was nimble enough, and could get about with speed. When she spoke it was in a cracked voice, like the croaking of a raven, so that her very tones caused the flesh to creep, and a shudder to pass through the frame of the listener. The nobleman would have passed on with a brief salutation, but the hag planted herself firmly in his path, and sawing the air with her forefinger commenced to speak.

"Thou art a proud man, Lord Lovel, and like all thy class thou regardest the poor as dirt beneath thy feet. But I tell thee that the hour is at hand when thou shalt be lower than they. They that live by the sword shall e'en perish by the sword, and they who scheme to entrap others shall be caught in their own net. The curse of doom is already on thee, and this night I can prophesy the end. Thy downfall shall be speedy, and thy death paltry. Nothing heroic shall there be about either. And the end shall be total. Neither child nor kindred of thine shall rule after thee in Longdendale."

Lovel heard, and, despite his courage, he could not help trembling at the terrible aspect of the witch.

"Out upon thee, thou whelp of Satan," he said at length, "or I will have thee in the ducking stool."

But with a shriek of horrible laughter the witch vanished.

Now this was the end of Lord Lovel, and the reader may decide for himself whether or not the witch's prophesy was fulfilled. It is quite certain that from that date his fortunes began to wane. He fought in the Battle of Bosworth Field on the side of the defeated King Richard III., and after the battle he took refuge for a time in Longdendale and Lancashire, but finally was forced to fly to Flanders. He returned to England with the Earl of Lincoln as a supporter of the Pretender, Lambert Simnel, and was a prominent figure at the "court" held for a brief space by that would-be King at the Pile or Peel of Fouldrey—now a picturesque ruin on Fouldrey Island off the coast of Lancashire. On behalf of Simnel he fought in the Battle of Stoke, and the last seen of him was after the defeat of the rebel army, when he was observed to join in the flight, and to swim his horse across a river, and to scramble safely up the further bank. Some say he was slain in this battle, but the popular version of his death ascribes to him a far different ending. According to this version some days after the combat, the disguised figure of a man might have been seen wending his way stealthily to a house at

Minster Lovel, near Oxford. The fugitive was none other than Lord Lovel himself.

With his enemies on his track, and afraid to trust even his friends, he made his way alone to his own house and entered it under cover of the darkness. Then, not daring to trust even his oldest servants, lest they might be tempted to betray him, he quietly stole to a secret underground chamber, and there immured himself, thinking to lie hidden within until he could find some means of escape from the country. What actually happened no man will ever know, but it is easy to surmise. It would appear that Lovel, from some cause or other, was unable to open the door by which he had entered his hiding-place, and having told no one of his intention to make use of the chamber—or else through treachery—he was perforce left to his fate, and died of starvation. In all probability when he found out his predicament he attempted to set some record of it down on paper, but, if so, his story was destined never to be read. He disappeared from the sight of his own generation, and the world had well-nigh forgotten him. But in the Eighteenth Century—several hundred years after his death—a party of workmen broke into the remains of an underground chamber at Minster Lovel, and to their great surprise came across a skeleton. It was thought that this skeleton was the frame of the once powerful noble—Lord Lovel.

It is said that when the workmen broke into the vault, the skeleton was found sitting at a table, the hand resting on a bundle of papers, but that with the admission of air it soon crumbled into dust.

After the Battle of Stoke, Lovel's lands were confiscated, and in 1409 were granted to Sir Wm. Stanley, who had turned the fortunes of the day at Bosworth Field. With this change of ownership Longdendale passed out of the hands of the Lovels for ever.

XII

The Raiders from the Border-Side

THERE was once a time when it was considered the height of fashionable conduct for the Scotch who lived upon the border, to dash into the Northern Counties of England, put the men they met with to the sword, burn their homesteads and stores, and carry off the women and cattle. It is quite true that the English, on their part, considered it fit and proper to cross the Scottish border, to raid the lands, and carry off women and cattle from the lower shires of "Bonnie Scotland;" and so on the score of fairness neither side had any cause for complaint. But then, both parties never thought of that; the nature of their own conduct was never questioned, it was always the other side that was in the wrong. Their opponents were "thieves and marauders," their own forays were characterized by the high sounding title of "military expeditions." For such is the way of the world.

There is no record to say whether the men of Longdendale ever rode north to join in expeditions across the Scottish border; but it is chronicled that "bold moss-troopers from the border-side" occasionally raided as far south as the rich country of the Longdendale valley. These Scotchmen usually came in strong and well-armed bands, consisting of picked fighting-men, and, oftener than not, led by some distinguished lord or knight who wished to reap fresh honour by reddening his blade in English blood. Sometimes the lord or knight looked upon it as a fair (and certainly the easiest and cheapest) way of securing a wife, or mayhap a mistress, together with a good fat dowry in the shape of plunder. None can blame him for holding such views, for it all came in the manner of living in the olden time.

But it did not always happen that the raiders were successful. Sometimes the "raided" were on the look out, and the surprise party themselves met with a surprise.

It was a bright morning in the summer, and the valley of Longdendale had never looked more beautiful than it did that morning when Jock, the steward's son, kissed his sweetheart at the end of the lane ere he entered the woods to join his father's men, who had some work to do in the forest. A fine lad was Jock, merry and free as becomes one whose life is mostly spent in the greenwood: his limbs were finely made, he was straight and strong, and there were none in all the country-side who could run, fence, or box like he, or who could shoot straighter or further with the bow. A right proper lad, such as an English maiden loves. His father was steward to the Lord of Mottram, and to that position young Jock looked one day to succeed. In the meantime he discharged such tasks as were set him with diligence, and drank his fill of happiness with that bonny yeoman's daughter, Bess Andrew. Bess knew his habits and his times of departure and homecoming right well, and thus the two found many a chance to bill and coo throughout the day.

It was with a light heart that Jock sped through the lanes when he had taken leave of Bess; and with a heart as buoyant, sweet Bess returned to the homestead when the parting was over. The maid sang a snatch of a country song as she entered the farmyard and set about her tasks, wondering whether her mother had missed her during the few moments she had been absent in the lane.

BESS ANDREW

But Goody Andrew, the farmer's wife, was busy in the kitchen, and the farmer himself was away in the fields. His lands were broad, and on this merry morn he was busy at a distance. So Bess had the farmyard to herself save for the presence of the children, her brothers and sisters, all younger than herself.

Bess busied herself with the milking-cans for some time, dreaming, as sweet maids will, of love and hope and the life that is to be. Suddenly she started, then bent her head to listen. On the wind came the sound of horses' tread, and the jingling of harness; the sound increased in volume, and it came from the lane which led to the farm. Bess left her work, and moved to the gate. Then she screamed and turned to fly to the steading. For, all gay and boldly, armed to the teeth, came galloping into the farmyard a band of fierce moss-troopers, having at their head a tall big-limbed laird, from the Lowlands over the border.

"The raiders," screamed Bess, as she hurried towards the house. "God 'a mercy on us."

But she never reached the door, for the leader of the band rode to her side, and with a laugh leaned down, seized her in a strong grip, and swung her to the saddle before him.

"The raiders," echoed he; "and of a truth we have won a prize worth raiding. Come, kiss me, my beauty. Thou shalt be my share of the plunder."

He forced his face to hers, but the maid fought fiercely, and struck him in the face, whereat the trooper laughed again.

"What a spitfire of a wench" said he. "But we will tame thee ere thou art much older. Bring hither a rope my men, and tie her up. Also gag her until she has found her senses, and knows where and how to use her tongue. Now get to work and lose no time, for I have no wish to bring a hornet's nest about my ears. Ho! who comes here. Settle them off in the good old fashion."

The last words were uttered as a couple of farm-hands came from an out-building to see what was astir. The poor knaves were instantly seized before they had chance to cry aloud, and in another moment were hanging by the neck from a neighbouring bough. That preliminary accomplished, the troopers proceeded to plunder the farm of all its valuables, and to get together the cattle that lay about. Poor Goody Andrew begged hard for mercy, but her plea only met with a coarse laugh from the robbers.

"Thou art a well-favoured vixen," quoth the chief. "And had'st thou only been a score years younger, then I had not left thee to the embraces of the southerners. But thy daughter is fair enough, and I doubt not she will like her Scottish lover when her good humour returns. Now, my lads, set the stead ablaze, and then to horse."

The men obeyed to the letter, and in a little while the farm was blazing fiercely, the troopers, loaded with plunder, were galloping towards the hills, on the saddle of the chief was the lovely form of the maiden Bess, bound and gagged; and in the farmyard sat the good dame with her younger children, wringing her arms, and weeping bitterly.

In the distant meadows, Yeoman Andrew paused at his work to wipe the sweat from his brow, and then looked up. In the direction of his home a column of smoke arose, which had not been there when last he looked.

"Hallo!" quoth he, "there is surely something amiss. What ho! ye knaves, leave your work awhile, and hurry with me to the farm, for I fear the worst."

Then, in company with his men, he ran to the steading, to find his weeping wife, and the ruin of what had been his home.

The farmer was a practical man, so he just swore a good round English oath, and then he got to business.

"Ho, there! Will Leatherbarrow, do thou slip for my good grey mare down to John the smith's, get aback, and ride for thy life on their trail. Send word by any messengers thou canst catch from time to time, how they fare. And thou, Hob, cross the fields, and set the great bell at Mottram Church a-ringing, and the rest of you scatter and bring out the archers and the men who can fight. Cease thy chatter, good dame, and see if thou canst scrape me a good meal together 'fore I set about paying my debt to the Scottish laird."

In a little while the great bell at Mottram Church was clanging out its wild alarm, and from the woods and fields about, and the distant farms, the stout yeomen were hurrying into the town, bringing with them their bows and bills, their swords and axes, and their horses all ready for the chase. For they had ridden on the track of the raiders before.

As the men mustered round the cross near the church, a horseman galloped into the throng, the flanks of his steed white with foam. It was the first messenger from Will Leatherbarrow, who hung like a sleuthhound on the trail.

"They have e'en ta'en the Kings' high road," he shouted, "and they ride for the hills."

"They will turn off at the bend before they reach Glossop town," said Jock, the steward's son, who now sat his horse at the farmer's side. "I know a short cut, and we may head them off. Do you, Farmer Andrew, ride on the trail, and I will lead a band to get before them. Then not a man of them shall escape."

"To horse!" cried the yeoman, curtly assenting. And in another moment the spurs were driven deep, and the men of Longdendale were hard on the track of the foe.

Grim men were they when the scent of war was in the air. Men who had learned the use of the bow from their cradle. For did not the men of Longdendale help to scatter the French at Cressy and Agincourt, and did they not in later days join in the annihilation of the Scotch at the fight of Flodden Field? On they rode, and as they went, their number was swollen by fresh recruits, and so they galloped till near the sundown.

"The pace tells on the beasts," said one man at length.

"It will tell more on the Scotch," said another, "since they are hampered with plunder."

And the cavalcade still galloped along.

The road wound up the hills, and at the top there was a level stretch of several miles. As the band of pursuers reached the top of the rise, they beheld a cloud of dust at some distance ahead, and a shout of triumph burst from their lips.

"They are yonder!" said one. "Ride faster, my men. We shall catch them at the gorge."

"They will never get beyond the gorge," said Farmer Andrew quietly. "Jock will ambush them there. The thieves are fairly caught."

Then silence reigned again, save for the sound of the galloping horses and the rush of the wind about the horsemen.

The pursuers clearly gained upon the foe, but the latter reached the next dip of the road well ahead, and disappeared from sight. A few minutes later, when the Longdendale band reached the top of the descent, a glad sight met their eyes. Across the narrow path, just where the road bent, Jock had drawn up his men, and already the archers were at work. Already several of the Scotch lay dead upon the road, and the rest were in confusion. Ere they could rally, with a wild shout the pursuing yeomen burst on them at the charge, and then there was a fray well worth the telling. It only lasted a few minutes, and Jock backed out of it the moment he found the sweet maid Bess safely in his arms. But the rest of the Longdendale lads laid lustily about them until the work was done. A palatable work it was to them—a clashing of blades, a crashing of axes, and then the great Scottish raid was over. Yeoman Andrew was avenged, and he had more in plunder from the Scots than made up the total of the damages he had sustained.

It is said that many a "guid wife" in bonnie Scotland looked southwards with eager eyes for the homecoming of her "man" from the foray in Longdendale, but always looked in vain. For the ravens had a rich feast spread on the hills above the Derbyshire and Cheshire border, and those Longdendale moors were dotted white with the bleaching bones of Scottish men.

XIII

The Legend of Gallow's Clough

NEAR Mottram, on the verge of the moors, overlooking what is now the high road to Stalybridge, is a spot known as Gallow's Clough, which, as its name implies, was in feudal times the scene of the Gibbeting of malefactors. Here in the good old days, was reared the gallows, whereon the criminal was first "hanged by the neck until he was dead," and from which his body was afterwards suspended in chains, until the weather and the birds between them had picked the flesh away, and nothing remained but a few bones—a grim reminder of the power of the law, and the folly and risk of departing from the paths of virtue.

In the days when gibbetting was fashionable, it behoved almost every petty township to possess its own gallows, for there was far too great a demand for the services of rope and hangman to permit of only a few recognised places of execution, and one common hangman, as is the custom at the present time. Not that people were very much worse than they are now, but the extreme punishment of the law was meted out for what are now considered the minor crimes of sheep and cattle stealing, poaching, highway robbery, house-breaking with violence, and such like offences. The sight of a dead man dangling between earth and sky was of too common a nature to cause surprise, even so late as the early decades of the nineteenth century.

Wild and lonesome as the Gallow's Clough is at the present day, it was a much bleaker and more awesome place in the days when the gibbet was standing there. Then it was considered as a place accursed, and was said to be haunted by the ghosts of all the dead men who had been strangled there. Even in the daylight folk gave the spot a wide berth, and at night when the winds moaned down the gullies from the hills, and swayed the dead men to and fro, and caused the chains to clank and rattle, then, indeed, the traveller kept as far off as his route would permit, and hurried past with beating heart, and face blanched with fear.

78

Nor was that all the terror. Witches were said to infest the place at certain seasons, and in the darkness to hold converse with the ghosts of the malefactors, from whom they learned how to transact deeds of darkness successfully. Men forced to pass that way at these seasons had seen from a distance the crouching forms of the old hags, and had even heard their crooning voices, and the fiendish laughter with which they accompanied their terrible midnight revels. Many a timid dame added a petition to her prayers—that Providence would accord her and all belonging to her, special protection from the witches who danced and plotted and sang the hell-song round the gibbet at Gallow's Clough.

On a certain day in the olden time, a throng of people might have been seen wending their way through Mottram to the place of execution at Gallow's Clough. It was a gloomy procession,—calculated to depress the beholder for the remainder of the day, and probably for many days to come. First marched a company of well-armed men—part of the retinue of the feudal lord—and in their midst was one bound, and wearing a halter dangling from his neck. Behind came a motley company of the country-folk—some weeping, some grimly silent, and some few laughing and jesting. Most of those who thus followed in the heels of the armed men were women, and in the front rank of these was a handsome peasant girl, who wrung her hands and cried aloud as though distracted.

The prisoner—condemned man though he was, with only a few hundred yards between himself and death—walked with a firm tread, and head held proudly erect. Now and then he turned his head to look at the weeping, wailing girl, and at such times his eyes grew moist: when the guards somewhat roughly thrust the girl back, his lips compressed, and his chest heaved, and his arms tugged at the thongs which bound him, in a manner which indicated that it would have fared ill with the guards had the young man been free. But beyond those silent manifestations of feeling, the prisoner marched to his death as calmly and fearlessly as though the journey had been an ordinary country walk.

Presently the procession reached the gibbet at Gallow's Clough, and here it halted. The guard cleared a space about the gibbet, and by means of their axes and bills kept back the crowd. The prisoner and the executioners took their place beneath the gallows, and near them stood a well-dressed man—the representative of the feudal lord.

Without loss of time, and with but little ceremony, the executioners went about their business, heedless of the cries of the women, and the piteous appeals for mercy from the handsome peasant girl.

Soon the preparations were complete; the well-dressed, officious-looking personage drew forth a document, and proceeded to read aloud the details of the crime for which the poor wretch had to suffer death—shooting at and killing deer in his lordship's forest of Longdendale—a crime of so serious a nature in the eyes of the authorities of that day that nothing less than the death of the offender could atone for the sin. The reading being ended, the reader nodded to the executioners, and they made as though to carry out the sentence forthwith.

But at this juncture a diversion was created, for the young woman who had hitherto so persistently and closely hung upon the steps of the guard, burst through the ring and threw herself upon her knees before the lord's representative.

"Mercy, mercy, Master Steward! Thou canst save him yet; and it is such a little crime. What is one deer from the forest against the life of a good man? He but shot the deer because I—his wife—and his child needed food. And if thou sparest his life we will work, and more than doubly make up the loss to his lordship."

The steward—a dark man of evil countenance—looked at the girl for a moment, and hesitated; then he caught the eye of the prisoner, and instantly his face grew stern.

"Get thee gone, thou baggage," said he, spurning the female. "Stop her mouth, some of you; or, if she will scream, take her to the ducking stool."

Then, turning to the hangman, he curtly said:

"Do your work."

With a wild cry of despair, the girl sprang up, leaped towards the condemned man, flung her arms about his neck, and kissed him, and then, before any could stop her, burst from the crowd and fled, shrieking and laughing, over the wastes of the hills. In another moment the prisoner was dangling in the air, and before the night fell the gibbet at Gallow's Clough held the ghastly form of a dead man swinging in chains.

It was midnight, and the skies were inky black; not a single star showed in the heavens, and there was no moon. A cold wind moaned down the gully, and swung the dead man in his chains so that the gibbet rocked and creaked. In the distant farms the timid country folk shivered in their beds, and as the wind shook the casements, they trembled the more, and told each other they could hear the clanking of the chains and the shrieking of the witches at Gallow's Clough.

It was a night on which few would care to stir out of doors, but for all that there were those who set out through the eerie darkness to wend their way to the gibbet. When night had fallen, the dead man's wife crept down from the hills and stood beneath the swaying form of her lifeless husband, and with a grim energy cast pebbles, and uttered shrill cries to scare away the birds that came to peck at the carrion that had once been man.

As she kept her vigil, she sang snatches of wild songs, and ever and anon talked to the dead man as though he could understand. It was clear that the woman's grief had driven her mad.

Towards midnight she slackened in her exertions, and seated herself at the foot of the gibbet, contenting herself with fearful but intermittent screams to scare away the birds. But presently nature gave out, and she fell into a troubled slumber. She was awakened by the sensation that some other mortal was near, and with a wild cry she sprang to her feet to find herself confronted by an old hag who appeared to be sawing at the dead man's wrist, as though to sever the hand from the arm.

"Malediction," croaked the hag, "who art thou?"

"I am his wife," answered the mad woman. "What dost thou want, witch?"

"Ah!" said the hag; "now I know thee. Thou hast need of help and friendship—I will be thy friend."

"What dost thou here?" said the woman, unheeding the latter part of the sentence.

"I seek a dead man's hand, and a dead man's flesh. The hand I would dry and wither in the smoke of the fire, and it will point out the way by which my schemes may achieve success. Of the fat of the dead man I would make candles—witch-lights—and by their glimmer I shall see, and see, and see,—things and secrets that are hidden from mortal eyes."

"Thou shalt not touch this dead man; he is my husband. Seek what thou requirest elsewhere."

The witch placed a long hand on the distracted widow's shoulder.

"Be not so foolish, poor wench," said she. "Trouble not over what I do. I tell thee I am thy friend, and the hand of thy dead husband once in my possession, will be of more service to thee than if left rotting here. Will not the ravens come—the birds of the air—and peck the bones clean; and is that not a greater defilement than boiling the fat in the witches' kitchen, and drying the dead man's hand in the smoke of the witches' fire? Listen!—dost know the meaning of revenge?"

The poor widow's eyes glistened as though a fire burned within her brain, and she repeated the single word "Revenge."

The old witch laughed, and said:

"Ah—thou knowest that. Tell me thy story."

Then the younger woman told the tale of want and woe and cruel wrong.

"The steward cast his eyes on me," she said, "but I loved my husband, and would have nought to do with him. And one day, my man being near when the tyrant insulted me, struck him to the ground, whereupon the steward dismissed him from his post, and we were made beggars. Then my child sickened, and since we needed nourishment, and there was no chance of honest labour for my husband, he took to the forest and shot one of the deer, saying that no wife or child of his should starve as long as there were any of God's creatures to be shot in the woods of Longdendale. The steward heard of this, and, like a wicked fiend, he hounded my

82

man to death. There his body hangs, and the man who drove him to sin walks about in pride and power."

She ended her story with a wail, and commenced to tear at her hair.

"Where is thy child?" asked the hag.

The distracted creature pointed to a bundle, which she had previously deposited at the foot of the gallows. In the bundle was the form of a male child, lately dead.

"Dead too, like its father," said the witch. "How did it die?"

"It died of want and of grief. Grief poisoned my milk, and the child drank of it and died."

"Does anyone know 'tis dead?"

"No one but me—its mother."

The witch looked intently at the eyes of the mother, as though she would read her very soul.

"And thou would'st have revenge?" she asked at length.

"Would I not," answered the woman; "Oh, would I not. 'Tis all I live for now. Give me vengeance and I will become thy slave."

"Then listen to me." And the hag whispered something in the ears of her young companion which appeared to satisfy her, for in a little while the two left the gibbet, carrying the dead child in a bundle between them.

The next day, one who passed the gibbet noticed that the corpse hanging thereon had only one hand.

A short time afterwards it was reported that the infant child of the steward had been spirited away in the night. It had been set to sleep in its cradle, and when the nurse awoke the cradle was empty, and the window open. There was a great outcry, and men were sent in search; the searchers presently returned bearing the dead body of a male child, the face of which had been half eaten away. It was impossible to recognise the features, but the steward wept over the body, telling himself that his son had been devoured by some savage beast of the forest, that had made its way into the mansion, and stolen the child while the household slept. He suspected that some evil witch-wife had been at work, and he trembled with fear, for he was sore afraid of the powers of darkness, as all wicked men are.

Meanwhile the dead man's widow dwelt with the old witch at a haunted hut in the forest, and it was reported that her son throve apace.

Years passed by, and the steward had no more children. The shock of his son's death had proved too much for his lady's strength, and she became an invalid. He grew more brutal and unmerciful in his conduct day by day, and the peasantry came to regard him as a fiend in human shape.

As for the old witch and the poor distracted widow and her child, they lived in the haunted hut, shunned by all—for it was reported that the widow herself had also become a witch, and was in league with the powers of darkness. The lad grew up into a fine youth, and had he lived an honest life, he would have been accounted one of the handsomest and likeliest lads in all Longdendale. But the training of his mother and the old witch had led him to spend his days in all manner of evil, he robbed and plundered, and finally took to the woods as an outlaw. Inspired by his mother, he was particularly severe in his depredations upon the property of the steward, and being reckless and daring to an unusual degree, he had so far succeeded in avoiding capture. At length there came a time when an adventure more impudent and daring than all previous affairs, caused the steward to put a price upon his head, and so keen was the hunt after him that the bold rascal found it necessary to keep in hiding.

The steward chafed with anger, for all his efforts to lay the robber by the heels were fruitless, and he had small hopes of ascertaining the whereabouts of the man he wanted. One day, however, an old hag presented herself at his gate, and asked for an interview.

"Ah," said he, recognising the old witch, "what doest thou here. Where is that imp of Satan whom thou hast helped to rear?"

"That, good Master Steward, is even what I am come to tell thee," answered the hag.

"How now," said the steward; "what evil scheme is afloat now?"

"Revenge," said the witch, snapping her toothless gums, and shaking her crutch. "Revenge upon the woman—my companion,

84

and upon her evil-minded son. They have played me false, and now I mean to return the compliment. The woman is away on a journey, and to-night her son crept in from the forest for shelter and a meal. I gave him meat and drink, but I drugged the drink, and now he lies in slumber at my hut in the forest. Send thy guards, steward, and take him ere he wakes."

The steward rubbed his hands with glee, and laughed joyously.

"Thou devil's spawn," said he, "thou shalt be rewarded if we take him."

"I seek no reward but to see him gibbetted," said the witch.

"Thy wish shall be gratified," said the steward; and without more ado he called his men, and marched off to the witch's hut to effect the arrest.

In those days little time was lost between the arrest of a man and his death upon the gallows; and on the following day the witch and her companion—the young widow of the earlier part of this story—accompanied a procession to the place of execution at Gallow's Clough. The steward was there with his men-at-arms—and as he beheld the widow, he turned to her and began to rail.

"Ah, thou hell-cat. Dost thou love the gallows so? Thy husband died on this gibbet, and now thy son comes to the same end. Like father, like son. 'Tis in the breed. Why dost thou not weep and shriek for mercy as thou did'st when thy man was swung?"

Then the woman answered with a laugh:

"Because I am mad, thou fool, and cannot weep. My tears were dried up with weeping over my husband, and now I can weep no more. I must laugh, man, laugh when the gibbet creaks beneath the weight of a dead man. The days of weeping are past, the time of laughter and rejoicing is come."

"Thou speakest truth," quoth the steward, turning away. "Thou art mad indeed."

"Yet not so mad as thou, oh, thou wise man," said the woman,—but the steward did not hear her.

The executioners did their work, and the young man was hanged by the neck until he was dead. Then the steward and his men turned to depart.

But the widow stood before him, and laughed in his face.

"Wise man—madman, rather," said she. "Whom, thinkest thou, is that dead man on the gallows?"

"Thy son, witch, thy son," said the steward, stepping back before the wild appearance of the woman.

"My son, fool! Nay, 'tis thy son, steward. The child who disappeared from his nurse's room was brought to me, was reared by me, was trained for the gallows, and hangs there dead. My son died the same day that his father was hanged—murdered by thee—and his mangled and disfigured body was found by thy servants and buried as thy son. Dost understand me now?"

The steward reeled, but recovered himself with an effort.

"'Tis false," said he, in a choking voice.

"'Tis true," screamed the woman; "was not there a birthmark upon thy child's shoulder? Ah, thou rememberest it, I see. Look at the dead man on the gallows, and thou wilt find the birthmark there."

With a wild cry the steward stripped the clothing from the dangling corpse, and there upon the lifeless shoulder, he found the mark which branded the criminal as his child. He had hanged his own son.

Before his men could lend a hand to stay him he had fallen senseless to the ground.

The men turned and sprang towards the woman, who was now convulsed with horrible laughter.

"Seize her," cried one,—and they all made to obey.

But quickly raising a phial to her lips, she drank the contents, and in an instant fell back a corpse.

The old witch shook her crutch at the armed men.

"The murder of an innocent man is avenged," she cried. "Is it not written that the sins of the fathers shall be visited upon the children? And lo—the murderer's son perishes upon the gibbet where the father's crime was done."

Then, laughing shrilly, she hobbled away over the hills, and, full of fear, the men-at-arms let her go unmolested.

XIV

The King's Evil

Or The Wonderful Cure of the Mottram Parson

THERE was a certain John Hyde appointed Vicar of Mottram in the year 1575, who continued to hold the sacred office for over 50 years. He succeeded his father, Sir Nicholas Hyde (the Vicar of Mottram from 1547 to 1575) who was buried in the Chancel of Mottram Church on the 24th day of April, 1575. John Hyde married at Mottram on February 26th, 1575-6, Alice Reddich, of Mottram, by whom he had several children: and after her death on March 21st, 1593-4, he married for a second wife, Ann Hyde, on May 22nd, 1597. In the year 1599 the Parish Registers were transcribed from the old paper books into the parchment volumes now in use, and every page of the transcripts bears the signature of John Hyde. He was also rural dean of Macclesfield.

During a great portion of his life, Parson John Hyde had curates to assist in the discharge of his ministerial duties; this assistance was the more necessary on account of the wide extent of the ancient parish of Mottram, and also because there was a chapel at Woodhead dependent for its ministry upon the mother church at Mottram. The most prominent of these curates was his eldest son, Hamnet Hyde, who, as appears from the Mottram registers, was baptized at Mottram Church on May 14th, 1580, and afterwards settled in the town, marrying there on the 12th day of January, 1601, Joane Greaves, of Mottram, by whom he had three sons, John, Nicholas, and Thomas.

Parson Hyde was of an ancient family of gentry, notable in both Lancashire and Cheshire; being connected with the Hydes of Denton, and the Hydes of Hyde. His great influence, however, was not alone owing to this circumstance, but was rather due to his own attainments and his proved superiority in the matter of learning and wisdom. Hamnet Hyde, his son, inherited his father's good qualities; he was a man of good parts, was distinguished for his learning, and was withal pious and devout. He made a good curate in every way. He was well liked by the parishioners of Mottram, and was, indeed, well spoken of throughout the whole of the Longdendale country. It should also be added in view of the details of this tradition, that he was a fairly robust man, steady, sober, in no way given to gluttony, and there seemed every prospect of his living to a good old age.

There came a time, however, when good Master Hamnet Hyde was greatly distressed to find a grievous disease slowly yet surely creeping over him. Do what he would, it was impossible to shake the sickness off. Bit by bit the disease grew worse, and the local quacks and surgeons were entirely powerless to stay its course. One by one the local doctors tried, and each one was sorrowfully obliged to confess to failure in the end. "Nothing could be done," they said; and a complete cure seemed almost hopeless.

Now, not only was Master Hamnet Hyde distressed with this intelligence, and not only did his good wife Dame Joane, weep until her good looks were impaired, but the news also gave great pain throughout the parish. The people took the matter to heart as though the parson was one of their own relations. So greatly was he beloved by the common people that some of them even went so far as to employ charms and other harmless means, whereby they hoped to remove the sickness from which the curate was suffering.

The curate's condition formed the subject of gossip when the people gathered together about the cross opposite the churchgates after divine service.

"Goodman Shaw," said one to his neighbour, "what think you of Master Hamnet Hyde to-day?"

The man addressed shook his head sadly before he answered.

"Methinks we shall not have many more sermons from him unless he alters greatly."

The curate, it should be stated, had preached that morning.

"Thou art right, goodman," went on the first speaker, "but it comes into my mind that there is one remedy he has not yet tried, which it were worth his while to put to the test. Someone should suggest it to him."

"And what is that, pray?" "Why, the Royal Touch. Let him visit the King, and be touched for the evil. There was a pedlar called on my dame but yestereen, and he told a great tale of the marvellous cures wrought by His Majesty King James, God bless him. Why should not our curate journey up to London, and get the King to remove his sickness?"

"Why not, indeed. Thou hast spoken wisely."

It should be mentioned that in those days the cure of disease by the patient being "touched" by the Royal fingers was widely believed in. It was asserted that kings were specially endowed by God with the power of healing by touch; and of all the monarchs who ever ruled in England, none were believed to have received this truly royal gift in such abundance as that Most High and Mighty Prince, James the First.

A suggestion of the sort mentioned by the gossip was not likely, therefore, to be neglected, and accordingly the idea was laid pertinently before the curate, who eventually made up his mind to seek the royal remedy. With this object in view, he mounted his horse, and, attended by his friends, journeyed southward to see the king. Before setting out on the journey, he commended himself to God, for the roads were infested with highwaymen, and it was a perilous venture to travel from Longdendale to London at that time. There was a goodly congregation in the old church at Mottram, and from the heart of every worshipper there went up a fervent prayer for the curate on the occasion of the last service specially held before his departure.

On the morrow the whole village was early astir, for it was known that the curate would that morning set out upon his journey; and a numerous array of villagers gathered in the street before the parson's door as the hour of departure drew nigh.

"Fare thee well, good Master Hamnet," cried one; "God prosper thy journey."

"If the king but touch thee thou art surely healed," said another.

"Look well to thy pistols, parson," quoth a third. "'Twere a pity not to put to good service the weapons God hath placed in our hands. And, of a truth, there be many rogues upon the road."

89

MOTTRAM CHURCH AND VILLAGE CROSS

"Be sure the beds whereon thou sleepest are well aired," put in an old dame. "Nothing aggravates the sickness like a damp bed."

And so with numerous manifestations of good will, the sturdy Mottram folk sped their parson upon his journey.

Now, after safely passing the many perils of the road, Master Hyde arrived at Greenwich in due course and, securing an audience of the King, was touched by His Majesty upon the 22nd day of May, 1610. There was a crowd of sufferers gathered about the Royal Palace, many of whom, like the curate, had travelled from a distance, and they cried aloud for joy when the King came amongst them. They fell upon their knees before him; and, with a gracious smile and many words of comfort, the monarch passed through the crowd, touching each patient as he passed, and breathing a prayer for their welfare. Immediately the fingers touched the patient, the royal virtue passed into the frame of the sufferer, and he was instantly healed. Then the crowd gave thanks to God and his Majesty, and with glad hearts set out for their homes.

It is needless to dwell long over the homecoming of good Master Hamnet. The news of his return was heralded abroad, and when he entered the village, the people flocked about him, throwing up their caps and cheering lustily, so that he returned like some great conqueror to his own.

After his return, he not only showed his gratitude by rendering public thanks to God for the wonderful cure performed upon him, but in order that future generations might know of the Divine goodness, and the King's most excellent kindness, he inscribed the following passage in the parish register of Mottram, where it may be read to this day.

"Anno Dni, 1610. Md. that uppon the 22nd daie of Maie, 1610, I, Hamnet Hyde, of Mottram clerke was under the King's most excellent Matie. his hands (for the evill) and att Greenewiche was healed. On wch. daie three years itt is requyred by his Matie. that the ptie so cured shoulde returne (if God pmitt) to render thanks bothe to God and His Matie.

God save Kinge James, p. me. Hamnettum Hyde, clericum."

Hamnet Hyde lived several years after this miraculous cure. He died in 1617, and was buried at Mottram on the 3rd January, 1617-18. The entry in the register written by his father is as follows:

"1617-18, January 3rd. Hamnet Hyde, my sonn, buried—."

Parson John Hyde survived his son Hamnet nearly 20 years, for he continued Vicar of Mottram until the year 1637, being buried on the 17th March in that year. He left direction concerning his burial in his will as follows: "In the name of God. Amen. The 13th February, 1633, I John Hyde, Vicar of Mottram, in the County of Chester, Clerk, being aged. My body to be buried in due and decent manner under the stone where my late father lyeth buryed, in the Chancell of the Parish Church of Mottram, adjoining to the tomb of Mr. John Picton, late parson there," etc., etc.

91

It may be added in conclusion that the sovereigns of England claimed and frequently exercised the power of healing certain diseases by touch. The curing of scrofula, or the "King's Evil," as it was called, was practised by Henry VII, Henry VIII., and Queen Elizabeth; and was also very extensively carried on by those believers in the "Divine Right" theory—the Stuart Kings. The "cure by touch" was believed in as late as the time of Queen Anne. The "Form of Healing" occurs in the older prayer books, especially those of the 17th century.

XV

The Magic Book

THERE is a spot prettily situated near the town of Glossop, known as Mossey Lea. It is notable as having been the home of a great magician, who dwelt there in the olden time, and who was renowned far and wide. He was, perhaps, the most learned and powerful of all magicians who have lived since the days of Merlin, but unfortunately his name has been forgotten. Such is fame.

So renowned was he in his own day, however, that pupils came to him, not only from all parts of England, but even from across the seas. These pupils desired to be inculcated with the mystic lore, and invested with the same degree of skill in the exercise of the magic arts, that their master possessed. Accordingly they left no stone unturned in their efforts after knowledge—that is to say, they were not over-particular as to the means they adopted to secure the end they had in view. They strove to impress upon everyone with whom they came in contact, their vast superiority to ordinary mankind, and generally they proved a big nuisance to the country side.

But there were two of these pupils who were especially curious; they were constantly prying into nooks and corners which were labelled "private"; they were ever meddling with business that did not concern them. By some evil chance, the magician fixed upon these two pupils to act as his agents for the transaction of some business in a town in Staffordshire, and to bring back with them a very remarkable book, which dealt with magic, and which was, moreover, itself endowed with magical powers. Thus the two luckless youths became all unwittingly the heroes of the following Longdendale tradition.

History—as is often the case in these legends of the olden time—has forgotten to record for us the names of the two notable youths, hence we are driven to the necessity of naming them ourselves, in order to distinguish them from each other. So we call one Ralph and the other Walter. It has already been said that they

93

were two curious youths, ever ready to pry into things; and on the night preceding their journey, they indulged in this pastime to the full.

While they were at supper the magician had bidden them to repair to his private chamber ere they retired to rest; and having entered therein, they were treated to the information already recorded—namely, that they would have to make a journey on his behalf, transact some business, and bring back with them a magic book—with the addition of the following piece of advice and warning.

"Look to it that ye heed what I now say," said the magician; "for by the shades, 'tis a matter of mighty import. Ye shall get the book, and ye shall jealously guard it. On no account shall you open it. More I do not vouchsafe to you, but remember my warning. Open not the book at your peril. Now get ye to rest, for to-morrow you must een start with the rising of the sun."

The youths left the room looking very solemn and good, with many promises that they would faithfully remember their master's charges, and what was of more consequence, that they would act upon them. But for all that they did not retire to rest. When they reached the passage leading to their apartment, Ralph said to Walter:

"What thinkest thou of this quest of ours? Is our master treating us fairly in thus keeping secret this matter? We have paid a high fee for tuition in magic, and here he sends us on our first quest, and we are een to know nothing of the mission on which we go."

"Thou art right," said Walter. "'Tis most unfair, and methinks our master has in view the acquisition of some potent power. If we engage in the quest, it is but fair we should share the spoil—the knowledge to be gained."

To which Ralph added, "I am with thee, comrade. And I would know more of this business before I start."

Here he whispered to his companion, and the latter nodded his head in acquiescence. After which the two stole together in silence to the door of the magician's room, and in turn set their eyes to the key-hole, whilst their ears drank in every sound.

The magician was seated before a crucible, muttering certain incantations which are as foreign language to the unlearned. But the two students understood the meaning of the sentences quite well, and the result of their eavesdropping appeared to give them satisfaction. When the magician made signs of coming to the end of his labour, they skipped nimbly away, and sought their beds, chuckling triumphantly as they ran.

It is not to the purpose of the legend to dwell upon the incidents of their next day's journey. Suffice it to say that on that day they were early astir, that they went gaily upon their way, and in due course received the magic book from its owner. Then they set out on their homeward journey, looking very good and innocent until they were well out of sight. But withal both determined to see the inside of that volume before the day was over.

Soon they came to a lonely part of the country, and here they sat down, intending to gratify their curiosity.

"If there is knowledge contained within, then am I determined to drink of the well thereof, and become even one of the wise."

So spoke Ralph, and Walter also said:

"And I am of a like mind, comrade. So bring hither the book, and let us fall to."

They placed the thick volume upon their knees, and quickly undid the handsome clasp which held the sides together, when, lo! a veritable earthquake seemed to have come upon the scene. The ground shook, houses tottered, walls and fences fell down, a tremendous whirlwind arose, which uprooted trees and tossed the forest giants about like little wisps of hay. Even the students were terrified at the result of their curiosity, and as for ordinary mortals, why there is no describing the panic in which they were thrown.

When the luckless students recovered from the first shock of astonishment, they could only bemoan their folly in discarding the warning of so potent a magician as their master, and they were filled with dread as to the punishment they would receive when next they stood before him.

"Of a truth we are undone," said Ralph; "our master will never more trust us."

"We are like to be beaten to death with the tempest," said Walter "Who can stay the power of this evil Spirit, that our mad curiosity has thus let loose?"

Now, luckily, the magician no sooner beheld the tempest than he at once divined the cause of this hubbub of the elements, and with commendable promptitude he proceeded with all speed to the spot where the students lay with the magical volume. Arrived there, he pronounced an incantation, and then by magic means known to himself alone, rapidly stilled the tempest, which the ill-timed curiosity of his pupils had brought forth. In the words of the old chronicle, he "laid the evil spirit, commanding him as a punishment to make a rope of sand to reach the sky."

Which venture no doubt had a salutary effect upon the spirit, for there is no later mention of any similar antics on its part. We may conclude from this circumstance, that the spirit has found the task assigned it as a punishment, greater than it can discharge, and that it is still labouring away at the sand rope, which is not much nearer reaching the sky than it was when the work first begun.

XVI

The Parson's Wife

IN olden time Providence often punished the sins of men and women in some remarkable fashion. The divine retribution often followed swiftly upon the violation of the sacred rules of life. We frequently read of profane men and women whose blasphemy has been instantly followed by some paralytic seizure, or who, when guilty, and protesting their innocence have called down heaven's vengeance on their heads if they were not even then stating the truth, have been at once rendered lifeless by some strange stroke of the divine power. The following story will illustrate this principle.

There was once a parson of Mottram—his name and the date of his holding the benefice are for obvious reasons not mentioned—who had a peculiar wife. In many respects she was a loveable woman, but she possessed a nose formed like a pig's snout, and she was forced to eat her meals out of a silver trough specially provided for her. How she came to win the affections of the parson, is not known, it might have been that she had riches to make up for her deficiency in beauty of countenance, or it might have been that the parson saw in her compensating charms which were not obvious to the rest of mankind. This tradition only deals with the cause of her strange infirmity.

Her parents were very wealthy; her mother was a haughty dame who worshipped wealth, and looked down on all people who were humble in station. To those wealthier than herself, or whose social standing was above her own, she was most polite and agreeable, and willing to go to any trouble no matter how great, to win their friendship and esteem, but to those who were poor, no matter how estimable they might be in mind, ability, or real worth, she was chilling and distant, and even insolent in bearing. True Christian love and charity were virtues she did not understand. Probably she did not believe in them; at least she did not practice them. No poor man's blessing ever ascended to heaven on her behalf, for she was never known to bestow a gift willingly upon the needy. So, no doubt, Providence considered that it was necessary she should be taught a severe lesson, that thereby mankind might be led to see that such un-Christian conduct was opposed to the highest rules of life, and could not be practised with benefit and impunity.

One day, to her door, there came an old beggar woman and her children, clearly betokening by their appearances the utmost misery and destitution. Their clothes were all in rags, only just able to hang together, while here and there, through the great rents, the flesh showed bare and cold. Their faces were pinched, and their frames thin and withered from lack of proper food; and nearly all of them were shoeless. Their feet were red and blistered, cut in places by the sharp stones of the wayside.

"A charity, I pray, good lady, for the love of Christ," said the beggar woman as the lady stood at the door. "Not a bite have we had this day, and we have travelled far. If thou hast children of thine own, take pity upon the starving children of the poor."

But the haughty dame bade her begone.

"Out on thee, thou vulgar drab," said she. "Thou art no honest woman, else had thou hadst a husband to provide for thee."

"My man is dead, lady," protested the beggar, "and I am left a widow."

"More likely thou art a harlot, and the children basely begotten. Away with thee from my door, or I will have the constables after thee, and thou shalt be publicly whipped for a low woman."

Then, losing her temper completely, she called for her serving men.

"Ho, there. Rid me of this pest. Turn out this old sow and her litter, for there is the smell of the stye about them."

At this outrage the poor woman fled. Some say she called down the vengeance of heaven upon the haughty dame, others state that divine justice asserted itself of its own accord. Be that as it may, the wealthy lady was in due course with child, and she brought forth a daughter having a face shaped like an animal with a pig's snout thereon, who in after years married the parson of Mottram. Thus did pride and want of charity bring its own reward.

XVII

The Devil and the Doctor

LONGDENDALE has always been noted for the number of its inhabitants devoted to the study of magic arts. Once upon a time, or to give it in the words of an unpublished rhyme (which are quite as indefinite)—

"Long years ago, so runs the tale,
A doctor dwelt in Longdendale;"

and then the rhyme goes on to describe the hero of the legend—

"Well versed in mystic lore was he—
A conjuror of high degree;
He read the stars that deck the sky,
And told their rede of mystery."

Coming down to ordinary prose, it will suffice to say that the doctor referred to was a most devoted student of magic, or, as he preferred to put it—"a keen searcher after knowledge"—a local Dr. Faustus in fact. Having tried every ordinary means of increasing his power over his fellow mortals, he finally decided to seek aid of the powers of darkness, and one day he entered into a compact with no less a personage than His Imperial Majesty, Satan, otherwise known as the Devil. The essentials of this agreement may thus be described.

It was night—the black hour of midnight—and the doctor was alone in his magic chamber. He had long desired power sufficient to enable him to accomplish a certain project, and hitherto all means by which he had tried to secure that power, had been of no avail. Blank failure had attended every effort, and at last he had decided to make use of the most certain, yet withal most desperate, agency known to him. In other words, he would call up the Prince of Darkness, and ask his aid. The only thing which troubled the doctor was the thought that the price which Satan would demand, might be much greater than he would care to pay. But, after all, that was something he would have to risk.

He set a lamp burning on the table, and into a small cauldron hung above it, he poured certain liquids, which he mixed with certain evil-looking powders and compounds. Some of the items which he added to this unholy brew, appeared to have once been members of the human frame. But that, of course, was known only to the doctor. When the brew began to simmer, the doctor commenced to mumble certain strange incantations, which he continued with unabated vigour for the best part of an hour, without, however, eliciting any manifestations from the dwellers in the spirit world. At length, however, his patience was rewarded, for the light beneath his cauldron suddenly went out, the mixture within boiled over, and the vapour which rose from it, spread over the room until all the objects therein were hidden as though by a thick black cloud. Then, out of the cloud, came a voice, deep and terrible in tone, which caused the very building to rock as though an earthquake had occurred.

"Why hast thou summoned me from the shades, O mortal, and what dost thou require?"

The doctor gasped with awe, he almost felt afraid to address the dreadful spirit, which his own incantations and rites had brought from the underworld. At length he screwed up sufficient courage to proceed, and said:

"I would have the possession of certain powers, O, thou Dread spirit."

"And of what nature are they?" asked the spirit.

Whereupon, the worthy doctor commenced a long explanation, into which we need not enter, setting forth his evil desires, and begging the Devil to aid him.

"Thou shalt have all that thou requirest, and more," said the Devil when the doctor had come to an end of his requests; "that is, providing thou art prepared to pay the price."

"And the price is?" ventured the doctor, trembling.

"The usual one," said the Devil. "I have but one price, which all mortals must pay. On a day which I shall name, thou shalt wait upon me, and deliver up thy soul to me."

"'Tis a stiff price, good Satan," said the doctor in protest.

"'Tis the only price I will listen to," said the Devil.

"Then I must een pay it," said the doctor, seeing that further argument was useless, and, being by this time quite determined to have his desires no matter what the cost. "I agree," he added. And there and then he signed the bond in blood, with a pen made from a dead man's bone.

Satan pocketed the bond.

"Thy desires are granted," said he. "Make the most of thy opportunities. One day I shall surely call upon thee for payment."

Then, with a burst of mocking laughter, he disappeared.

The doctor seems to have enjoyed the results of the compact until the day drew near for the settlement. Then, indeed, he appears to have repented, But he was by no means a dull-witted individual, and in a happy moment he began to cudgel his brain for some way out of the difficulty—some plan of escape. Before long his face brightened, a gleam of hope shone on it, and at length he seemed to see his way clear. He received the formal summons of Satan with a knowing smile, and when the day at last arrived, set out in good time to keep his unholy tryst.

In the language of the rhyme,

"Now rapidly along he sped
Unto a region waste and dead,
And here at midnight hour did wait
His Sable Majesty in state."

The Devil appeared, seated upon a coal black charger, which was of the purest breed of racing nags kept specially for the Derby Day of the Infernal Regions. Satan was very proud of his horse; he was open to lay any odds on its beating anything in the shape of horse flesh that could be found on earth.

Judge then of the Devil's surprise when the Longdendale doctor offered to race him. (It should be stated that the doctor had ridden to the place of meeting on a horse which was bred in

101

Longdendale, though the trainer's name has unfortunately been lost).

At first Satan laughed at the impudence of the proposition, but after some little haggling, he at length agreed to the doctor's conditions. The conditions were that the Devil was to give the doctor a good start, and that the latter was to have his freedom if he won the race.

"A RUNNING STREAM"

"I am unduly favouring thee," said the Devil; "I do not as a rule allow my clients a single minute's grace when payment falls due, and I do not reckon to let them bargain as to other means of payment. But for all that, I do not see why I should not make merry at thy expense. I am not altogether as black as I am painted. And if it will give thee any comfort to imagine thou hast a chance of escape—why then get on with the race."

Acting upon the above agreement, a start was made, and the course was along the road now known as Doctor's Gate. The contest was most exciting. Prose can scarcely do justice to the occasion, but we will endeavour to give some account of the strange contest. The Devil good naturedly conceded a big start, for, of course, he felt quite certain of reaching the winning post first, and when the signal was given he went full cry in pursuit. Away the coursers sped like wind, the doctor riding with grim countenance, and teeth firmly set, ever and anon casting an anxious look behind him, and now looking as anxiously in front. Meanwhile the Devil rode in approved hunting fashion, with many a loud halloa, which made the very mountains shake as though a thunder peal was sounding. His horns projected from his head, his cloven feet did away with the necessity for stirrups, and he lashed the flanks of his coal black charger with his tail in lieu of a whip.

Slowly but surely the Devil gained upon the doctor. Inch by

inch the black steed drew nearer the Longdendale hack, until at length the Devil, by leaning over his horse's head, was able to grasp the tail of the doctor's horse. With a loud burst of fiendish laughter, Satan began to twist the tail of the Longdendale horse, until at last the poor beast screamed with pain and terror. This greatly amused the Devil, who twisted the tail all the harder, so that the doctor's horse, goaded almost to madness, plunged along faster than before, and in its fright took a mighty leap into a running stream which dashed brawlingly across the path. All too late Satan saw his danger; he held on to the beast's tail and tugged with all his might. For a second, the contest hung in the balance, and the result seemed doubtful. But luckily for the doctor, the tail of the horse came off—torn out by the roots—the Devil's steed fell back on its haunches, and the doctor's charger plunged safely through the flood, and gained the opposite bank. Then the doctor gave a great shout of triumph, for according to the laws of sorcery—laws which even the Devil must obey—when once the pursued had crossed a running stream, the powers of evil lost all dominion over him.

Thus by a combination of skill, cunning, and good luck, the Longdendale doctor outwitted the Devil. Some profane mortals state that when he found himself victorious, the doctor turned towards the Devil, and put his fingers to his nose as a sign of victory, while the Devil, sorely disgusted, rode off to hell with his tail between his legs, vowing that the mortals of Longdendale would have no place to go to when they died, for they were too bad for heaven, and too clever for hell.

Author's Note

The road known as "The Doctor's Gate"—mentioned in the above story—runs across a portion of Longdendale. In reality it is part of the old Roman road from Melandra Castle, Gamesley, to the Roman station at Brough in the Vale of Hope.

With reference to the main incident of this legend, the following quotation from Sir Walter Scott will be found of interest:—"If you can interpose a brook between you and witches, spectres, or fiends, you are in perfect safety."

No date is attached to the legend.

XVIII

The Writing on the Window Pane

IT was an evening in the glad month of June, of the year 1644, and the children of Longdendale were playing games on the smooth green plots before the cottage doors. At one spot not far distant from the site of the old Roman station, Melandra Castle, a group of merry little ones, lads and lassies, were swinging round hand in hand, their sweet young voices chanting an old-time rhyme.

Suddenly there was a shrill cry from one of the girls, and following the direction of her gaze, the children beheld a sight that at first set their young hearts beating sharp with fear. A company of horsemen, wearing wide-brimmed and much befeathered hats, with long hair hanging about their shoulders, rode jauntily past the greensward in the direction of the Carr House Farm. The horsemen were well armed, carrying swords and pistols, and bright steel armour shone dazzling upon their breasts. As the cavalcade moved on, the jingling of stirrups, bits, and harness, made a merry music that was well adapted to the martial scene. The children, though startled at first, soon recovered from their fright, and ran gaily to see the squadron pass by. Curiosity, in their case, got the mastery of fear. For those were what the historians term "stirring times," — days of war and tumult, of peril and death, of bloodshed and ruin, of suffering and horror; and well the children of Longdendale knew that the quarrel between King Charles and his Parliament had already made sad hearts and weeping eyes, widowed women and orphaned children, even in their own neighbourhood. But the great battles of which they had heard had all been fought at a distance, and, as is well known in the case of war, "distance lends enchantment to the view." There was something wildly romantic and fascinating to the minds of the children in those great events which were daily transpiring, and about the men who fought in the battles; and so, on the June evening of this story, the children flocked curiously about the horsemen, who were a band of gentlemen cavaliers on their way from Lancashire to join the army of King Charles at York.

Accompanied by the children, the cavaliers rode up to the Carr House Farm, and, at a sign from their leader, dismounted, and, without troubling to ask consent, proceeded to stable their horses, and take possession of the best rooms for their own accommodation. It was not altogether a good mannered proceeding, but then, the people who lived in those days when war was rife, grew accustomed to such violations of the rights of property, and submitted to the indignities with as good a grace as they could assume. They knew full well that if they had not placed upon the table of their very best, the soldiers would have raided the larder and confiscated all the contents. So, in the language of modern days, "they made the best of a bad job."

One stalwart trooper, throwing the reins of his steed to a comrade, was the first to stride through the farm door, and, as he came, the farmer went bareheaded to greet him,—not altogether without some qualms of doubt and fear.

"Come, good man," cried the trooper merrily, "show me the way to thy best room, for our leader, Captain Oldfield, rests there this night. And if thou art of the King's party, set thy wife to work at once, and prepare him a feast right merrily, or if thou be'st of the roundhead faction, why, do the same unwillingly, and be damned to thee."

History does not tell us which side of the quarrel the farmer favoured, and it does not really matter which, for in any case a visit from the Royalists would be alike unwelcome. If he was a Roundhead, then, as a matter of course, the billeting of a force of Cavaliers was bound to be distasteful; if he were loyal to the King, then against the satisfaction of providing for the King's troops, must be set the knowledge that the next force of Roundheads that came into the neighbourhood would pay him a visit and demand satisfaction for the favour he had shown their enemies. The farmer made a discreet remark.

"If ye are true men, ye are welcome to such hospitality as I can afford."

And then he and his servants set about doing with as good a grace as possible that which they knew themselves compelled to do.

But although the soldiers might be unwelcome guests to the farmer and his wife, their coming was by no means received with a bad grace by other members of the household. The maids, in particular, seemed quite glad as they beheld the Cavaliers enter the yard, and what was more remarkable, they made scarcely any attempt to prevent the arms of the fighting-men stealing around their trim-set waists with the coming of the gloaming and the shadows. There were shy giggles and blushes and many a stolen kiss in and about the Carr House Farm that night, before the bugle sounded the hour of rest.

When all the men were inside save the sentries, whose duty it was to give notice of the approach of Roundheads—if any such rebel gentlemen should chance to put in an appearance—the officer in command gathered his soldiers around the oak table in the best room, and seated himself at their head. Captain Oldfield, of Spalding (for such was his name and title), first addressed the company, which included the master and mistress of the farm, and all the pretty maids whose lips so readily lent themselves to a soldier's kiss. He reminded his hearers of the great sin of fighting against the "Lord's anointed."

"For," said he, "did not God appoint kings and princes and governors, and if they are not to rule their people, wherefore are they created? Therefore it stands to reason that they who oppose the will, and set themselves in array against the authority of good King Charles, are fighting against God, and are likely ere long to suffer grievously from the displeasure of God. And I would especially urge upon ye good people of Longdendale that ye remain loyal and true to His Majesty, and have nothing to do with traitorous rebels who are prompted of the devil. So shall ye escape a felon's death here and damnation hereafter."

Then, drawing from his finger a ring set with a large diamond, he continued—

"My stay will doubtless be short, yet would I leave behind a loyal sentiment which shall serve to remind you of your duty toward your royal master."

106

Whereupon he advanced to the window, and on one of the little diamond-shaped panes, he scratched the following words in the Latin tongue:—

"May King Charles live and conquer.
Thus prays
John Oldfield,
of Spalding,
1644."

The task of writing being ended, he then called on all present to fill their cups with the farmer's best country wine, and drink deep to the sentiment which he had just inscribed.

The men filled their cups and drained them to the dregs, after which they cheered for King Charles. And then the band broke up, the troopers seeking their hard couches, while Captain Oldfield retired to his room with the officers, to discuss their future movements, and to question and gossip with the farmer and such of the loyal gentry of the neighbourhood as had come to greet him on hearing of the arrival of his force.

"And whither march ye, Captain Oldfield?" asked one of the gentlemen of Longdendale, as the talk went on.

"Toward York, Sir Squire," replied the officer; "To join the King."

"And how will the fight go? Think you the rebels will attack the city?"

"That I doubt. For Rupert is there, he of the Rhine, a Prince of fire, whose hot blood can never wait in patience for an assault. Rather should I think he will sweep down on the Roundheads before they muster in force sufficient to attack the city. As for the end of the fight, why, look you, I am no prophet. Being in the struggle I do my best, and I take the outcome, be it what it may, as becomes a true soldier. There be some who pretend the seer's gift of sight so that they can foresee what is to happen, but on such things I set little importance. If the end is evil, why, then, the knowledge of it comes soon enough. And if good, why the joy is all the greater for the waiting."

The farmer now raised his voice:

"If it please you," he said, "there is a neighbour woman who possesses the gift of sight. She foretells events in a manner right wonderful. If your worships like, I will e'en summon her before you."

"Well," quoth the Cavalier, "I have no objection to witnessing her antics, though I set no store by what she may say. So bring her within; 'twill help the time to pass."

The farmer left the room, and presently returned, leading in an old beldame, whose withered and bent form seemed scarcely able to stand upright. She leaned heavily upon an old crutch, and her breath came in loud gasps as though she were a prey to asthma.

"What is your will?" she asked, in a fit of coughing. "I am old; could ye not let me rest a'nights without summoning me to make sport at your revels."

"Come, granny," said one of the gentlemen, "be not ill-tempered; we would let these good Cavaliers witness a sample of your skill. They ride to York to join the King, and would know what fate awaits them there."

The old dame laughed shrilly.

"Better had they wait. Evil comes soon enough. Why not drink and be merry while ye may?"

"Why, granny, whence this croaking? What ill-fate seest thou?"

"I see what ye in your pride deem impossible. Ye have just now drunk to the King. Ye have inscribed on the window-pane of this dwelling a prayer for his triumph. And a bonny sentiment it is that ye have written, ye bloody murderers of Englishmen. Upholders of a tyrant, think ye that the powers of the other world will ever smile upon your cause? Not so. Your cause is accursed. Never shall the words of the writing come to pass. King Charles shall perish. So shall ye, his myrmidons. Lo! I see a field of battle. Rupert is there and the army of King Charles—a glorious array without the walls of York. But there cometh Cromwell, the man of iron, his horsemen charge once twice, thrice, and lo! the army of the King is scattered, and the earth is red with blood. I see faces, cold and dead, turned upwards towards the sky. The faces of men slain in the battle. And behold, some of the faces are your faces, For such is your doom. And in the end your King shall perish, and old England shall be free."

The frame of the old beldame shook as she delivered herself of this tirade, and when she had ended she moved feebly to the door. The company remained still, too awestruck to stay her, and presently she had disappeared. The soldiers soon recovered their spirits, and joked gaily over the occurrence.

But it was destined that the words should come true.

With the first streak of dawn, Captain Oldfield led his men on their long march to the city of York. There on the second day of July, they fought in the Battle of Marston Moor, and, even as the woman had prophesied, most of the band perished in the battle, and Cromwell beat back the King's army, and England was one step nearer being free.

Author's Note

Ralph Bernard Robinson refers to the above legend in the following passage in his little book on Longdendale.

"Opposite, on the other side of the river, is Melandra Castle as the the villagers call it. Some fields here are called in old deeds 'The Castle Carrs.' Hard by is an ancient homestead going to ruin called 'The Carr House.' This old house has an historical celebrity. A party of Royalists, on their march to Yorkshire before the Battle of Marston Moor, stayed here one night. The name of the Captain, John Oldfield, of Spalding, that of King Charles, and the date (1644), long remained inscribed in Latin, with a diamond ring, on a window-pane of the old dwelling."

In some way or other, the pane of glass referred to by Robinson became the property of the late A. K. Sidebottom, Esq., J.P., and after his death was purchased at a public auction by my friend, Mr. Robert Hamnett, of Glossop. To the kindness of the last-named gentleman, I am indebted for the loan of the glass, and for various particulars concerning it. When it came into Mr. Hamnett's possession, it was in two pieces, which, however, have now been cemented together. The pane is the ordinary size of small diamond panes frequently found in cottages of old date, and still largely used in the windows of our churches. The inscription is quite clear, but the glass is badly scratched, as though some sturdy member of the Cromwell faction had done his best to obliterate the Royalist writing without going to the expense of breaking the window.

The inscription is as follows: —

> Vivat et vincat Rex Carolus,
> Sic orat
> Johnes Oldfield
> de Spalding
> 1644.

Mr. Hamnett has been at considerable pains to trace the career and family of the above John Oldfield. I am indebted to him for the following particulars. The passage given here is taken from an ancient MSS. belonging to the family, and has been supplied by the Wingfields, who are direct descendants of Captain Oldfield.

"We now come to John—the Captain Oldfield of the Longdendale legend—the eldest son of the first Anthony, who, as we have sayd, succeeded to his estate November, 1635. This gentleman was a most zealous Royalist, and as the other party prevailed (he being left wealthy by his father, notwithstanding his providing so well for his other children), was at several times plundered by the parliamentarians, and sequestred as a Delinqt., and at the Siege of Newark, where he served the Royal cause gallantly as a gentleman volunteer, was shot through the body, but recovered of his wounds. He married Alice, the daughter of — — Blythe, of Shawson, in the County of Lincoln. He added to, and very much improved the seat built here by his father, building the rooms and grand staircase in the north wing of that house, and planting many forest trees and much wood about it. This John was interred in the chancel of the Parish Church of our Lady and St. Nicholas, in Spalding, as was Alice, his wife, by whom he had three sons and as many daughters, viz., Anthony, his eldest, who succeeded him to his estate and was afterwards created a Baronet by King Charles II.... We now come to Anthony, eldest son of John, who, as we have said, succeeded to his father's estate, 1660. He married first Mary, the daughter of — — Parker, Esq., by whom he had no issue; secondly, Elizabeth, daughter of Sir Edmond Gresham.... This gentleman was much esteemed and had a great intimacy with people of the greatest worth and quality in his neighbourhood, and particularly with Sir Robert Carr, Bart., Chancellor of the Duchy of Lancaster, and one of His Majesty's Most Honble. Privy Council, and upon the recommendation of the Rt. Hon the Countess of Dorset, he was, by His Majesty King Charles II., by letters patent, bearing date the 6th day of August, 1660, advanced to the degree and dignity of a Baronet of England, by the title of Sir Anthony Oldfield, of Spalding, in the County of Lincoln, Bart.—he lies in the chancel under a very large grey marble, upon which is this inscription:—

"Here was interred the body of Sir Anthony Oldfield, of this town, Bart., who departed this life the fourth day of September, Anno Salutis—1668; Aetatis—42."

Sir John Oldfield, son of Sir Anthony, married in 1668, but at his death in 1704, left only three daughters surviving. The baronetcy accordingly became extinct. Elizabeth, the third daughter and co-heir of the last Sir John, married John Wingfield, of Tickencote, High Sheriff of Rutland (1702). From this union spring the present family of Wingfield, which includes among its members Sir Edward Wingfield, K.C.B., and Captain John Maurice Wingfield, of the Coldstream Guards.

XIX

A Legend of the Civil War

IN the year 1644 the town of Stockport became the scene of some exciting incidents in the great struggle then waging between the King and his Parliament. From ancient days, Stockport had been accounted a place of military importance, commanding, as it did, the passage of the river Mersey. When the Romans took possession of the county, they established a strong fortified camp upon a site near the modern market place. The Norman lords of Stockport reared a castle upon the same site, and from that period downwards, the strategic value of the place continued to increase. When the Civil War broke out, the importance of obtaining and maintaining possession of the town, was soon recognised by both factions, and throughout the grim and prolonged contest. Stockport was held first by one party, then by the other, as the respective fortunes of the Cavaliers and Roundheads ebbed and flowed.

The majority of the principal landowners and gentry—that is to say, the most powerful of the representatives of the old county families—in the vicinity of Stockport, were much inclined to Puritanism, and so the cause of Parliament received strong support in this part of the country. The Bradshawes of Marple Hall were vigorous supporters of the Roundheads—Colonel Henry Bradshawe was a distinguished Parliamentary soldier; and his brother, John Bradshawe, afterwards became President of the Council of State, acted as the Judge at the trial of King Charles, and passed the death sentence upon that unhappy monarch. The Ardernes of Arden Hall, the Dukinfields of Dukinfield, the Hydes of Hyde, and the Hydes of Denton were all resolute supporters of the Parliament; and inasmuch as all these families had property and influence in the town and parish of Stockport, it is scarcely a matter for surprise to find that in the year in which our story opens Stockport was held by a Parliamentary force under command of that staunch soldier, Colonel Dukinfield, of Dukinfield.

Colonel Dukinfield is a man who deserves a few words of description. He was one of the most distinguished of the group of famous historical characters who sprang from this part of East Cheshire, and helped to mould the destinies of the nation in the 17th century. A man of Puritan ancestry, himself a great Puritan, with Republican tendencies, endowed, moreover, with many of the gifts of a great soldier, he took part at an early age in the opening stages of the great war. His exploits in the field, and his influence and ability to raise and keep together strong bodies of horse and foot, soon won for him a high place in the ranks of the Parliamentary party; and right worthily did he acquit himself, whether in the field at the head of his troops, or in the Council Chamber, where all the qualities of a statesman were called into play. Historians are unanimous as to the disinterestedness of his character, and the purity of his motives; indeed, it is generally recognised that he was one of the truest men of either party that the Civil War produced.

In the year mentioned, he was sent to guard Stockport, and the bridge over the Mersey—one of the entrances from Cheshire into Lancashire—and this task he performed, until military necessity compelled him to evacuate the town, and retire before a superior force of the enemy.

A strong army of Loyalists, being sent to invade Lancashire, must needs take possession of Stockport on their way; they were led by that dashing dare-devil nephew of the King—Prince Rupert of the Rhine. Recognising that the enemy was too strong for him, and deeming it imprudent to risk the lives of his soldiers in a hopeless resistance, Colonel Dukinfield withdrew his force, and vanished from Rupert's sight. He of the Rhine sent his men through the rich farm lands about Stockport, and they plundered the suffering yeomen—confiscating whatever they required for the service of the King. The Roundheads, on their part, had done the same, so no one could grumble very much about the matter. As the sufferers said, "One side was every bit as bad as the other."

But not a glimpse of the Roundhead soldiers did the gay Cavaliers get, and Rupert of the Rhine, hot-headed as he was, had yet more sense in his pate than to be led astray from his direct line of march to begin a risky, fruitless, and possibly disastrous chase of the Parliamentarians. For he knew that Dukinfield, who, being a native, was acquainted with every yard of the country, had taken refuge in the wild and mountainous region of Longdendale, where it was easy enough for the Roundheads to ambush the Cavaliers, and where there was little chance for practising that dashing form of warfare—the grand charge of large masses of cavalry upon equally compact masses of the enemy—which was Rupert's favourite method, and which—until Cromwell and his Ironsides came upon the scene—was invariably successful.

So after a time Rupert passed on his march.

Our story, however, has to do with the troops of the Parliament, and their sojourn in Longdendale. When he left Stockport, Colonel Dukinfield led his men directly to the wild country beyond Mottram; and on the lands adjoining the old halls of Mottram, Thorncliffe, and Hollingworth, and about the homes of the wealthier inhabitants, he quartered his force. He does not seem to have met with much resistance in this matter; and it is most likely that the Longdendale landowners were themselves inclined to favour the Parliamentary cause.

Be that as it may, they found food for horse and men, and supplied Dukinfield with money, cattle, and soldiers, when the time came for him to march. There are some interesting documents still preserved, which give the details of the various expenses to which the Longdendale gentry were put by the prolonged stay of the Roundhead forces on their lands.

As was to be expected, the arrival of so renowned a fighter as Colonel Dukinfield, and his bold band of Roundheads, caused more than a flutter of excitement in the breasts of the country folk of Longdendale. Those inclined to the Roundhead faction, were rather proud to stand by and wave their caps and cheer at the brave men who had so resolutely fought against the tyrant King; while the Royalist inhabitants surveyed the soldiers and their Puritan colonel, with feelings akin to hatred seeing in them nothing but a set of rebels who were too vile to live.

Of the last-named class was a stout yeoman whom for the purpose of this story we will name Timothy Cooke. A thorough

King's man at heart, he had no sympathy with any who set themselves up to fight against the "lords anointed," and as he saw the Roundheads ride past he would, had he dared, and had the opportunity presented itself, have put a bullet into the body of each rider.

"A damnable set of psalm-singing rascals," muttered Tim to a companion, as the Parliamentary troops went by. "May the food and fodder they get in Longdendale, choke both man and beast. They are of the devil's spawn, every one, enemies to God as well as to the King."

"Steady, Tim," whispered his companion. "They will overhear thee, and then, belike, thou wilt get into serious trouble."

"Trouble!" quoth Tim. "I care mighty little for anything they can do. The King's forces will wipe them out ere long; and had I been but half the man I was in my young days, I would have ridden behind the Cavaliers, and struck a blow for His Majesty."

Then, grumbling at the perversity of the times, which permitted such unseemly sights as that presented by a band of Republican soldiers marching coolly through Longdendale, he jogged off homeward, to weary his wife with his ill-humour.

But the goodman had more to put up with ere long, for after a few days were passed, there came riding into his farmyard, the stalwart figure of a Roundhead. The soldier was a young man, of gentlemanly appearance, and strikingly handsome. He wore his hair cropped close, and his face was clean shaven. He sat his horse firmly, and his well-proportioned figure gave signs of strength.

"Farmer," cried he; "I give you a good day. You have a grey mare, I understand, of some little fame hereabouts. My officers require the use of her for the service of the Parliament. And I am come to take her forthwith. Also a sheep from your fold would not come amiss, but that you may send to the headquarters by one of your farm hands."

He spoke with the free air of one who expected that his requests, or orders, would be observed as a matter of course.

Timothy stood stock still for a few moments, lost in wonder. Then his hot temper blazed forth in a volume of words.

"Why you knave—you close-cropped murdering rebel—you

115

speak and carry yourself with the bearing of an honest King's man. Get out of my yard this instant, or I'll brain you on the spot. No horse or sheep of mine goes from here to the service of the King's enemies."

He flourished a large hay-fork dangerously near the horseman, and the steed began to back with alarm.

"Drop that fork," cried the soldier, drawing his pistols, "I've no mind that there shall be any accident, but if you will advance, and if one of these weapons goes off, 'tis no fault of mine."

But the old farmer's blood was up.

"I'll spit you as I would a goose," cried he; "and all other such Republican knaves."

The soldier pulled his horse aside, and levelled his pistol at the farmer's head.

"Thou mad fool," he cried. "If thou wilt rush to thy death, 'tis no concern of mine."

And sighting the weapon, he made ready to fire.

But at that moment came a diversion, and from an unexpected quarter; for in the doorway of the farm, directly behind the irate yeoman, there appeared the figure of a maid. She was the farmer's daughter, and a maid of uncommon beauty; and the sight of so fair a daughter of Eve, bursting thus suddenly on the soldier's vision, banished for one brief second the murderous purpose from his mind. He hesitated, let his eyes wander from the farmer to rest upon the figure of the girl. That second's hesitation was fatal, for the hay-fork driven with force by the yeoman, took him in the shoulder, and tumbled him heavily to the ground. He had a confused sense of having done something very foolish and unsoldierlike, of falling with a thud from his horse, of a sharp pain in the shoulder, and then his senses left him.

When he recovered consciousness, the unfortunate Roundhead found himself lying on a couch inside the farmhouse. He was at first dimly aware that a somewhat heated discussion was going on in one quarter of the room, and that some person with gentle touch bent over him and tended to his hurts. In another moment, his senses having fully returned, he could distinguish the

116

voices of the disputants, and knew that they were talking about himself.

The farmer's wife, good mistress Cooke, was denouncing her husband's folly in having wounded the soldier, and thus brought the man nigh to death, and the yeoman, himself, in grave danger of arrest, court martial, and the gallows.

"'Tis thy hot temper, of which I have so often spoken, and which thou never canst control, that has led thee into this mess—and a pretty mess it is, upon my conscience," said the dame, "What harm had the poor fellow done to thee or thine, that thou must prod him with the fork, as thou dost a truss of hay, and tumble him headlong out of the saddle. A mercy it is he did not break his neck by the fall. As it is, he is not seriously hurt, though the back of his head will carry a lump for many a day, and his shoulder will be stiff enough for weeks. The next thing that will happen, I suppose, will be that thou wilt have the whole band of them—foot and horse—about the house, and they will carry thee away a prisoner, and I and the bairns will een be tumbled out upon the road-side."

"Stop thy chatter," growled the farmer, his courage somewhat overawed by the volubility and sting of his wife's tongue. "Wouldst have me let a Roundhead knave, an enemy to the King, rob and plunder me of the grey mare, and a sheep from the fold, without using the hay-fork when 'tis in my hand. Death and damnation is too good for all such rogues."

..."Death and damnation," quoth the dame. "Death and damnation, forsooth. That is like to be thy reward for the business. Out of the room, man, for thy presence drives away my patience. Out thou goest, while I see if I can bring the poor fellow round, and make amends for thy fool's folly."

She bundled the farmer out, and at this moment the Roundhead opened his eyes. Then he shut them suddenly, as though some bright light had dazzled him, for there, bending close above him, was the bonny face of the maiden, whose dazzling beauty had been the cause of his undoing. She had been tending to his hurts, and was gazing at him anxiously, wondering the while if he were about to die.

The Roundhead did not long remain with closed eyes, for the

117

vision of the maid was too sweet to lose for want of the effort of raising his lids. He gazed straight into her eyes, and smiled; and the girl, finding him fully alive, and conscious of her presence, blushed crimson, and drew backwards in confusion. Her movement attracted the dame, who by this time had got rid of her husband; and having no special desire to be the recipient of attentions from an old lady—no matter how estimable and kindly disposed she might be—the Roundhead, with an effort sat up. He had not been seriously injured by his fall, which had done nothing more than deprive him of his senses for a short time; and the thrust in the shoulder was nothing more serious than a flesh wound; now that the bleeding had been stopped, he was really little the worse for his misadventure.

"I thank you, madam," said he to the farmer's wife, "for your kindness and attention. Doubtless your good offices, and those of the young lady, have saved my life; and I promise you they shall not be forgotten in my report to my commanding officer."

Relieved as she was to find the Roundhead out of all danger, poor Dame Cooke was terribly upset on hearing the concluding words of the soldier.

"Oh, sir," said she, the tears springing to her eyes, "must you indeed report the misdeeds of my hot-headed husband. If he is taken, and called to account for this mishap, I much fear that his punishment will be severe. If you could overlook—could find some excuse—could——"

She broke off, utterly unable to say more, but her eyes pleaded with the soldier.

Restraining an inclination to smile, with an effort, the Roundhead said solemnly:

"A bandaged head and shoulder must of necessity give rise to comment. And how can I escape from the necessity of a report? Moreover, there is the matter of the grey mare, and the sheep."

"They shall be sent to your camp within the hour," put in the woman eagerly; "and more likewise, if ye will only be merciful to my good man."

Other talk followed, but for reasons of his own, the Roundhead omitted to assure the dame as fully as she could have wished, that she should hear no more about the matter. It was not without a feeling of great trepidation that she listened to his last words of gratitude for her personal attentions, and witnessed his departure.

Mounted on his horse, he rode slowly down the lane, and not till the farmhouse had disappeared from sight—hidden by a bend in the lane, and a dip in the road—did he meet a single soul. Now, however, he reined in his charger suddenly; and he felt his heart beat quicker as he beheld the pretty maid standing in the road barring his path.

Off came his hat, with a sweeping bow, that would have done credit to a Cavalier; and he bent gallantly in the saddle to converse with the fair being who had waylaid him with the evident intention of speaking to him.

"Oh, sir," said the maid, her voice trembling with emotion, her face rosy with excitement and bashfulness; "you will forgive my father will you not? He is not a bad man, and if anything happened to him, it would break my heart, and my mother's also. Do not punish him, and mother and I will make amends in some way."

The Roundhead looked at the maid, then cast his eyes rapidly up and down the lane, and a twinkle of merriment shone in his glance.

"You are quite willing to compensate for your father's sins— to render a service if I pledge myself to silence on his misdeeds."

"I will do anything," said the maid, eagerly.

The Roundhead bent low in his saddle, until his face was dangerously near that of his companion. There was a look in his eyes which caused the maid to blush a deeper red, and set her heart pit-a-pat with a thrill of strange and joyous excitement.

"Then kiss me," was all he said.

The girl dropped her eyes a moment, then looked full into his, and finally raised her lips and kissed him.

"Now," she said, "remember your promise, and keep it."

Then with a mischievous nod of her head, that caused her curls to dance in the sun, she skipped out of his reach, and ran up the lane towards the farm.

He turned the horse as though to pursue her, but contented himself with calling after her, "Tell your mother not to trouble about the grey mare and the sheep. I will come for them myself—another day."

He doffed his hat, and the girl waved her hand; and then the Roundhead trotted off to explain in some cunning fashion how he had foolishly met with an accident, and if his colonel had no objection he would go for the grey mare and the sheep another day. The young man was a favourite officer with his superiors, and his colonel had no objection whatever, so the farmer heard no more about his attack upon the Parliamentary forager.

It is not to be supposed that human nature of the masculine gender, however much inclined to Puritanism, could, after having once tasted the sweet lips of the farmer's daughter, resist the longing for more of such delights. And so the Roundhead more than once or twice made his way towards the farm; and either, owing to his cleverness, or to the strangest coincidence, it so happened that he never returned to quarters without having held some converse with the maid.

In this way the time passed, and to the two lovers it seemed as though everything was sweet and fair, and as though war, and suffering, and death were not abroad in the land. Indeed, so far, the revolution had brought nothing but fortune to the young man, for he was already promised a captaincy when next the troops were put in motion; and then he would move onward to fresh adventures, wherein he hoped to add to his laurels, so that when the wars came to an end, he would have a position of some standing to offer to his bride.

At last there came a day when Colonel Dukinfield bade his men make ready to march. Messengers had ridden in on foam-flecked steeds, and it was understood that great events were about to transpire. The troops looked to their arms, burnished up their breast-plates, and head pieces, and after a busy day spent in preparations, made ready to pass their last night in Longdendale in the fashion that the Puritan soldier loved.

When the night had fallen, groups of soldiers were gathered within the best rooms of the farms whose owners—being favourers of the Parliament—had gladly welcomed and billeted the Roundheads, and the host having brought forth some musical instruments, which were tuned up forthwith, soon the voices of all were joining in a Puritan chant of praise. Loud and long that night sang the Puritans, and ever and anon, in the intervals between the chants, some of them, in nasal tones, would break out into prayer— strange old-fashioned petitions, in which the Lord was asked to strengthen the arms of the Parliament, and to sweep the Royalist faction away as the leaves are scattered before the wind. Then with the first break of day the bugles sounded; and, leaving the fair Longdendale land behind them, the Roundheads passed to scenes of grim contest—some joining in the conflicts in Yorkshire, others participating in different sieges in Lancashire and Cheshire. After their departure, Longdendale was visited in turn by bands of Cavaliers, who rode towards the points of strife; and then for a time the valley was left to its rural quietness.

For some weeks the maid heard nothing of her lover and her only consolation during his absence was to chat and talk with the wives and sweethearts of Longdendale men who had joined Colonel Dukinfield's troops, and ridden off to the fight.

One day, however, when the tasks about the farm were all done, she sat in the old-fashioned seat in the advanced porch of the steading, which looked out towards the west. It was the close of a glorious day, and far away over the great levels of the Cheshire plain, the sun was setting—flooding the earth and sky with a light that seemed too beautiful to be real. It was as though one looked right into the gates of heaven. The farmer and his wife were seated near, for they, too, were weary with the toil of the day, and were resting for a space in the cool of the evening before the darkness fell.

Suddenly the girl raised her head as though to listen, and then pointing towards the sunset, she uttered a loud scream.

"There, there! do you not see them? the Roundheads are beaten back, and their leader falls. It is he, my love—and oh!—they have slain him——"

Then she fell back into the seat and sobbed, and shivered, and moaned.

The farmer took her by the shoulders, and shook her.

"Art daft, my lass," said he, "or dreaming. What is it thou see'st?"

For a moment the girl could not do anything but sob and moan, then, recovering herself, she told her parents that, as she gazed at the sunset, it seemed as though the western heavens were alive with the figures of men—she could see the Roundhead troops rushing to the assault, at their head was the form of her lover, and even as she looked, the Royalists repulsed the attack, and in the melee she saw her lover fall, his brain pierced by a musket ball. It seemed, too, that she could hear the noise of the piece, and the death-shriek as he fell.

"Tut-tut," said the farmer, "'tis nothing but a dream. Thou hast been dozing, that is all."

The mother also tried to comfort her, and the two led her inside, but that night when the farmer and his spouse sought their chamber, the latter said in an awesome whisper:

"'Tis the gift of sight, good man. My grandmother had it; and I fear that the vision she has seen will prove true."

Some days passed, and nothing was heard of the great strife which waged beyond the valley; but one day a man, pale and thin from suffering, seated upon a jaded steed, rode wearily into Longdendale. Near Mottram town he met Yeoman Cooke, whom he accosted; and the latter looked at him with a start of surprise.

"Why, Jack, is't thee, my man?" said the farmer. "Bless me if I knew thee. Thou art just like a ghost."

"And I had nearly been turned into one, farmer," answered the man. "For I got a blow on my head in the fight just a week gone by to-day, which stretched me senseless; and other hurts about my body, have knocked out of me all the fighting for some months to come. 'Twas an evil day for Longdendale, and I trow that thy own home will be turned into a house of mourning by it. For this was how we fared. Even as the victory seemed assured, the Royalist rascals made a great rush, and by ill-luck our leader was shot dead, and other officers falling, we were beaten off. As for the Captain— well, I think he loved that lass of thine—King's man though thou art,—for in his breast, when we came to carry his body off, were

122

certain keepsakes which I have seen thy daughter wear. There was also a letter addressed to her, and I have it with me here. Thou wilt tell her that he died as a brave man should die, and that he was worthy of her love to the last. I must ride on now, for it grows late, and I have ill-news to carry to other Longdendale women besides thy wench. This is the worst side of war."

ARMS OF THE DUKINFIELD FAMILY

"One moment," said the farmer, placing his hand on the bridle of the other's horse, "When did this happen?"

"A week ago to-day," replied the Roundhead. "Just as the sun set; and it was too late to renew the attack that day."

With that the man rode on, and the farmer was left alone.

"The good wife is right after all," he said to himself. "'Twas second sight, and the lass has the gift. We must keep the matter to ourselves, or the folk will think she is a witch."

Then he set his face homewards, and walked off wondering.

The following particulars from old historical documents will give the reader some idea of the part Longdendale played in the Civil War; they will also afford evidence of the unrest which was the predominant feature throughout the country, in the days of the great Rebellion.

Earwaker, the learned historian of East Cheshire, quotes a series of accounts from the Harleian MSS. These relate to Hollingworth in the time of the Civil War, and are the accounts "made and sworn unto by several inhabitants of the Township of Hollingworth" in 1645. The following extract will serve as a sample of the contents of this interesting document.

The accompts of Alexander Hollinworth, of Nearer Hollinworth, in the above said Townshippe.

Imprimis: I paid to Collonell Duckenfield, the 15th day of Deecmber (1643), for pposicon money	500
Itm: The same tyme ye said Collonell had of me a bay gueldinge ffor to be one in his Troope, well worth	568
Wch continued in his Troope until Candlemas after, and then was soe spoyled that he was not able to do any more service.	
Itm: After the said horse was soe lamed I sent another horse in his roome, and a man to ride him, which horse hath beene in ye said troope ev since Candlemas after to this present tyme: the horse when I put him in was worth	8100
Itm: I was att charges for the man that did ride ye said horse sev'all waies above 40tye shillings	200
Itm: When Sr William Breerton marched towards Yorke wth Cheshire fforces ffor ye assistance of that County, there was 250 horse and rydrs quartered at my house; the damage I had by them in eatinge my meadowe, killinge my sheepe, and plunderinge some of my goods privily, and consuminge	1368

my victualls they found in my house, to ye value att ye least of 20tie marks

Itm: The damage I sustayned in quarteringe some of Captaine Rich horse and foote ye most pte of halfe a yeare Anno 1642 att the least	1000
Itm: The damage I sustayned in quarteringe div'se of Captaine Eyres Troope sev'all tymes in Ann 1642 and 1643 was att the least	500
Itm: In quarteringe some of Collonell Deukenfield souldrs, Major Bradshawes, and diverse others, the tyme when Prince Rupert came to Stockport, was att the least damages to me	368
Itm: In quarteringe of 18 Troopers of Sr William Breerton Companye when they marched towards Nottingham (as they said) about 5 or 6 weeks agoe	1100
Itm: I have mainteyned one musquetyer from the beginninge of theise unhappy warres, and never had the value of one penny towards the charge thereof from the Publique	2500
Item: I have been sometymes att charge of one and sometymes 3 souldrs more when any publique danger was, as div'se tymes into Darbishire, to Adlington, to ye raysinge of the siege of Namptwicke, wch I verily thinke cost me above 5 markes att the least	368

Sum   £8268

John Hollinworth, of Hollingworth, had a similar bill of £70 16s., and the Booths and the Bretlands also sought recompense for the expense they had been put to in buying arms and quartering men.

One other old document may be quoted.

On the 8th of December, 1653, Colonel Dukinfield and Colonel Henry Bradshaw sat at Stockport to prepare a list of pensioners in the Stockport division in connection with the civil wars. The list contained the following names: Ellen Wagstaffe, whose husband was wounded at Adlington; Catherine Goodier, whose husband was slain at Nantwich; Ellen Heape, of Tintwistle, whose husband was slain at Nantwich; Elizabeth, wife of Hugh Wooley, slain at Chester; Jane Cooke, whose husband was slain at Middlewich; John Wylde, of Disley, wounded at Worcester; Thomas Hinchcliffe, wounded at Worcester; Elizabeth Small, whose husband was slain at Cholmondeley; Joan Small, whose husband was slain at Middlewich; John Sydebotham, wounded at Cholmondeley; Margaret Whewall, whose husband was slain at Selby; The widow of George Hopwood, wounded at Middlewich; Randal Cartwright, wounded at Hanmore; Margaret Ashton, whose husband was slain at Lichfield; Ellen Benetson, wife of William Benetson, of Dukinfield, wounded at Chester, and died.

It will be noticed that several of the above are names of Longdendale men.

XX

A Tale of the '45

THE year 1745 was a noteworthy year in the annals of Longdendale. In that year the valley was roused to excitement by the doings of Prince Charles Edward Stuart, the young Pretender, who, at the head of a large army, marched through Manchester and Stockport on his road to Derby. Many of the male portion of the inhabitants of Longdendale walked into either Manchester or Stockport to see the army pass, and to catch a glimpse of the romantic figure which might one day sit upon the throne of England. Most of these sightseers returned home full of the grand picture which the Scottish army presented; they told a great tale of how the Prince forded the river at Stockport, that the water took him up to the middle, that he wore a light plaid, and a blue bonnet, in which was set a milk-white rose.

These accounts greatly interested the inhabitants of Mottram town, who, like most people, loved to hear of martial doings at a distance. The Mottram folk, however, were not so highly elated when, a little later in the year, they heard that portions of the flying Scottish army were likely to pass through their town during the retreat from Derby. They would gladly have had the soldiers play the part of the Levite of old, and "pass by on the other side."

"A murrain on them," quoth the sexton, as he sat in the ingle of the "Black Bull's Head"—that homely tavern perched on the hillside just beneath the graveyard of Mottram Church. "Why cannot they even travel back the same gait they came, and leave our good Mottram folk in peace? Like enough if they come, there will be blows, and who knows but what my trade will flourish mightily. And that will be the only trade that will flourish if they get to fighting on this side of the border."

The maid who was attending to the wants of the customers pricked her ears at the conversation, and as she filled the sexton's glass, she joined in with her sweet woman's voice.

"For my part I should be glad to see them march through

127

Mottram. They say that the Prince is a handsome gentleman, and brave as he is fair. One day he will be the King, and then, think what an honour it will be to Mottram, to have had his army billet in the town when he fought for his own. Moreover, as I hear, there be some of the best and bravest of the old families of Lancashire in his train, and we see too few of the real gentry hereabouts to throw away so fine a chance as this. As for the fighting, I see no sin in that when the good Prince but seeks to win back his own."

The sexton smiled at the maid's enthusiasm. He slowly charged his pipe, lit it, and when she had done, took the stem from his lips.

"You are a maid," said he; "and like all women, are easily carried away by a handsome face and a fine figure. And belike you are a supporter of the Stuarts. As for me, I am for King George. I know enough of the Stuarts never to wish them in power again. My grand-father was a youth when the great war was on, and he saw enough blood shed then through the follies of Charles the First to turn him and all his kin against the breed. I could tell you tales he told to me that would set your heart a sick at the very mention of a Stuart. And war is not the grand thing some folks think. It's all well when someone else gets the worry, and pays the price, and leaves to us the glory of it. But I've no desire to see my thatch blazing above my head, my goods and chattels carried off, and my earnings squandered to keep some hungry fighting man in trim."

John the smith now took up the tale.

"As for me, I'm a favourer of the Stuarts. The lad is the true King, say I, by all good right. But I'm heart and soul with you, sexton, in hoping the army of the Scots will keep clear of Mottram town."

And as the talk went on the speakers were divided on questions of politics, some siding with the Prince, others with the House of Hanover; but all alike agreed in hoping that the fugitives would give the Longdendale country a wide berth.

Military necessity, however, knows no law, and the Scotchmen came at last—big burly Highland men. They wore kilts, and carried claymores—for the most part they were bearded, unkempt creatures, men who followed their leaders with the blind faith of children. As soon as definite news of the retreat of the rebel army in the direction of the town became known, the householders of Mottram became greatly alarmed, and everybody grew busy in hiding his or her valuables, and in driving the cattle to places of safety. The farmers scattered about their fields, and horses, cows, sheep, and swine, were hurried into the hills, and there secreted as comfortably and well as possible. Even the poultry were collected, and hidden away, so that they should not become a prey to the hungry Scots. It is said that the sexton had a busy time among the graves, burying such pieces of plate as were owned in the neighbourhood; and in many other spots throughout the district the savings of the householders were committed to the ground.

Contrary to expectation, however, the Mottramites found the Highlanders a quiet, harmless lot of mortals, who did not seem desirous of reckless plunder. When they arrived they showed no disposition to take more than was absolutely necessary to provide for their needs, nor did they turn the people out of doors, and take forcible possession of the houses. During their short halt at Mottram, they roughed it with the best, killing cattle for food, and then (through lack of proper utensils) boiling the meat in hides skewered up at the corners.

BELFRY DOOR IN MOTTRAM CHURCH

The kilts of the Highlanders were what interested the people most of all, and the children would often flit about, in and out, near the legs of the soldiers, looking in awe at the strange petticoats for men, and the knees all bare and bony. Sometimes the men would take the children on their knees, and tell them stories of war and panic, of the charging of horse and foot, and of the glorious deeds of the great and brave. At which the children were greatly pleased, and could have listened all day long.

The soldiers did not camp together, but were divided into companies; one portion stayed in Mottram, but the bulk of them encamped near Hollingworth Hall. Some of the inhabitants took pity on the men, and treated them with great kindness, which appears to have been much appreciated by the rebels. On departing, one of the soldiers left behind as a mark of his gratitude a tinder-box—the most valuable possession he had—and this box was long preserved at Hollingworth Hall.

A noticeable feature about the coming of the Highland men was the excitement and pleasure it occasioned among the female portion of the inhabitants of Longdendale. The lasses in no way showed those signs of distress and doubt which were so evident in their elders. On the contrary, they dressed themselves in their best, became gay with ribbons, and by every art known to woman sought to enhance their many charms. Even in those days a soldier's coat was a magnet of attraction to a maid.

Among the rest was the pretty maid who had spoken to the sexton in the "Black Bull." She was a fair lass, of good figure, and winsome ways, and she was greatly admired by all the lads of Mottram town. One of these was one whom we will call Robin Shaw, on whom she seemed to look with favour; and already that handsome yeoman had come to consider her as especially his property. A sad surprise was in store for poor Robin when the Scotchmen came marching through the town.

Robin, young though he was, had strong views upon the situation. He was a staunch "King's man," and it was with no good grace that he beheld his lady love sporting the rebel colours as the Highlanders marched by. His cup of bitterness, however, ran over when, on the next night, he came across the faithless damsel strolling down a lane, where he himself had often made love to her, in company with a handsome youth who followed the fortunes of Prince Charlie.

It was an angry scene which followed.

Good Robin lost his temper, and in the most approved Longdendale fashion, then and there gave forth his opinion of the heartless conduct of his lady love, and the unjustifiable meddlesomeness of the soldier. The two would have come to blows there and then (for the Scot was quite as eager for the fray as his enraged antagonist) had it not been for the presence of the maid, who placed herself between them, and firmly decided against hostilities. As it was, she commenced an onslaught with her tongue, and the unlucky Robin, on whose head she poured forth her wrath, at last beat an ignominious retreat.

"I'll be even with you yet, you bare-legged rebel," he cried to the Highlander as he went.

And the soldier with a light laugh replied, "At your service, my friend, whenever you are ready."

But the fates were against their meeting for the present, for, eager to get back beyond the border before the English army, which was massing, should lay them by the heels, the Scots left Longdendale, and passed hurriedly northwards.

The day after they left, a fine figure of a man, equipped and ready for war, strode into the bar of the "Black Bull" at Mottram. It was Robin Shaw, and he sought the maid.

"Well, my lass," said he, "I'm off. I've joined the army for the north, and now I'll be on the track of the rebels. If I meet your Highland lover, there'll be blows, and the end will be that you'll have no difficulty to make a choice between us. If I live, I'll come back to claim you. One kiss now, and then good-bye."

Without waiting to see if the girl would give consent, he drew her to him in a grasp that would admit of no resistance, and kissed her. Then without another word he left the inn, and went swinging on his way.

The weeks passed, and the grey dawn broke upon the heath near Culloden, where the English and the Scottish armies lay. With

131

the dawn the Duke of Cumberland set out on his march, and shortly after mid-day the roar of the English artillery told that the battle had begun. All the world knows the history of that fight, how the fierce Highlanders, rendered desperate by the play of the cannon upon their ranks, burst into that wild and ill-fated charge which met with a bloody repulse; but there are personal details of the conflict that the world knows nothing of.

When the Highland line darted forward, there moved in the front rank a "braw" young Scot, whom one at least of the Royal troops welcomed with a shout of joy. For an instant the weight of the Scottish column caused the English regiment to waver before the impetus of the charge. But there was one man who never gave ground an inch—the Longdendale Loyalist—Robin Shaw. He had seen among the charging host the form of the soldier who had tampered with his love in distant Longdendale, and with a shout he set himself in front of his foe.

"Now, my merry rebel," he cried; "we meet again. We will settle old scores."

"Thou art welcome," cried the Highlander, crossing blades. "We fight for the love of a lass and—King James."

"For the love of a lass, and King George," said honest Robin Shaw.

And with that the fight began.

Now, Robin was no match for his foe save in strength. In skill of sword play, the Scot was greatly the superior of the two, and the result was not long in doubt. Before he knew where he was, Robin's blade was dashed from his grasp, and the sword of the Highlander thrust him through. Robin grew sick, and a mist rose before his eyes, but in the mist he could still make out the triumphant face of his foe. With teeth firmly set, he pulled himself together, and sprang at the throat of the Scot. In vain the latter drew back. Before he could draw his dirk, the Longdendale lad had him by the throat, gripping him like a vice. The men fell to the ground, rolling over and over in the struggle, but the grip of Robin never slackened, and at length both lay still. Another moment and the beaten wave of the Highlanders swept over them, and the victorious English charged past in pursuit. The battle of Culloden was fought and won; Charles Edward was beaten, and the Stuart cause for ever lost.

When the burial parties passed over the battlefield, they found two corpses firmly locked together—an Englishman run through the body by the other's sword—a Scotchman strangled to death by the grip of his foe. The dead man's grip might not be loosened, and they buried the bodies in one common grave.

So Robin and his rival lay down together in the last long sleep beneath the heather at Culloden, and away in merry Longdendale a fair girl watched and waited for a lover who never came.

XXI

The Haunted Farm

IN the township of Godley, on the fringe of what was formerly an unenclosed common known as Godley Green, stands an old farm, stone-built, of picturesque appearance. It is pleasantly situated a short distance from the turnpike road, from which it is approached by a country lane. Its windows command some beautiful views over the farm lands of Matley and Hattersley, which stretch away eastwards with many a clough and dingle, to the bleak hill country where the old church of Mottram stands out dark against the sky. The farm is said to occupy the site of an ancient hall, and old folk tell of the remains of mullioned windows, and a curious antique mounting block, which were to be seen there in the days when they were young.

Tradition says that the farm is haunted. In former times it was occupied by a family, the last survivor of which was an old dame, who is spoken of by those who remember her as being the very picture of a witch. She is said to have had a nose and chin so hooked that they almost met; and to have been very mysterious in her movements. Rumour had it that there was some treasure or secret buried in or about the farm, and that after the old dame's death, her spirit, unable to rest in the grave, commenced to wander through the farm at night, as though searching for something which was lost.

Various persons who have at different times resided in the farm—some of whom are still living,—have related strange stories of their experiences of the ghostly visitant. In the dead of night, the doors—even those which were locked—have suddenly opened, footsteps have been heard, as though some unseen being walked through the rooms and up the stairs, and then the doors have closed and locked themselves as mysteriously as they opened. Sleepers have been awakened by the beds on which they lay suddenly commencing to rock violently; and at times the bed clothes have been snatched away and deposited in a heap upon the

134

floor. The ghostly figure of an old woman has been seen moving about from room to room, and then has vanished. Fire-irons have been moved, and have tumbled and danced about mysteriously; pots and pans have rattled, and tumbled on the floor; and there has been heard a strange noise as though some one invisible was sweeping the floor.

In the early and the middle decades of the nineteenth century, the appearances of the ghost were of frequent occurrence, so much so that the farmer's family became accustomed to them, and beyond the annoyance and the loss of sleep which were occasioned, ceased troubling themselves about the visits. But for guests or strangers the ghost had terrors. The farmer's daughter had a sweetheart, and one night he paid a visit to his betrothed, and sat with her before the kitchen fire. Suddenly there came a gust of wind, there was a noise as though every pot and pan in the house had been broken, and every door was flung wide open by a mysterious and invisible agency.

"What on earth is that?" asked the young man, full of surprise, not unmixed with terror.

"It is only the ghost of the old dame prowling about," answered his sweetheart.

But the youth had seen and heard enough, and seizing his hat, he dashed outside and made off rapidly over the fields. Scarcely had he departed, when the doors shut themselves, and all was quiet as before.

Some time afterwards, the farmer engaged a farm-hand from a place beyond Charlesworth. The new man took up his abode and slept one night in the haunted farm. The next morning he came downstairs with blanched face and startled eyes.

"I have seen a boggart," said he; "the ghost of an old woman; and I think it must be my mother. On her deathbed I promised her to place a stone upon her grave; I have been too greedy to spare the money for the purpose. It must be her ghost come to upbraid me; and I cannot rest until I have placed the stone above her grave."

Never again would the poor fellow spend a night in the farm, but for years he walked to and from his home beyond distant Charlesworth and his work at the haunted farm.

Other farm-hands and servants were equally terrified by the strange noises and apparitions; and the farmer found it almost impossible to get anyone to remain long in his service. At length, so annoying did the ghost visits become that it was decided to call in the aid of some minister of the Gospel for the purpose of "laying the boggart." The Rev. James Brooks—the respected pastor of Hyde Chapel, Gee Cross, from 1805-1851—was asked to undertake the task, and he readily complied. Accompanied by other devout men, he spent several nights in the haunted rooms, reading passages from the Bible, and uttering prayers specially adapted for driving evil spirits away. The ministrations of the reverend gentleman were so far successful that the ghost did not again appear for some time, and its visits have not since been of such frequent occurrence as formerly. It was widely believed that had Mr. Brooks continued his visits and his prayers long enough, the boggart would have been effectively "laid."

As it is, the strange noises and visitations have continued, and are borne witness to by several persons. Between 1880 and 1890 the following strange thing happened. It was in the middle of the afternoon, when most of the household were out of doors, and there were only the farmer's wife and a boy, and girl within the house. Presently the mother went into the yard, and the youngsters, bent on mischief, rushed into the pantry for the purpose of feasting on the jams and honey which they knew to be there, when lo! they were suddenly startled by a loud and strange noise overhead, giving them the impression that some burglars must have got in the upstairs rooms by some means or other. Full of fear, they rushed for their mother, who boldly went upstairs, the children following at her heels. When they entered the room from which the noise came, they beheld the curious sight of an old rocking-chair, violently rocking itself as though some person might have been seated in it, and the rocking continued unabated for a considerable time. A farm labourer, who was called in to stop the chair, was too terrified to do anything, and finally the farmer's wife had to sit in the chair to stop it.

It is said that the old dame whose ghost haunts the place, died in her rocking-chair in that very corner of the room; and the belief was that it was her spirit, invisible to the inhabitants of the farm, which had set the chair rocking so mysteriously.

To add to the mystery and the uncanny character of the place, there is a certain part of the garden connected with the farm, on which nothing will grow. Time after time have the tenants endeavoured to cultivate this little spot, but always unsuccessfully. Some years ago human bones were dug up, and the secret attached to their interment is supposed to account for the sterile nature of the soil. The present tenant of the farm asserts that he has paid special attention to the piece of ground, has applied quantities of the best manure, and in other ways has endeavoured to bring the soil to the same state of fruitfulness as the rest of the garden, but all to no purpose. So recently as the month of April, 1906, primroses growing on that part of the garden are pale and withered; while those in other parts are fine and healthy flowers.

The present tenant's wife relates a strange story of a supernatural death-warning which occurred in connection with this haunted house. Her brother lay ill in the farm, and she had occasion to go to Gee Cross on business. Returning homewards, she met a black cat, which, do what she would she was unable to catch. Then, whilst walking along the lane leading to the farm, in company with her mother who had met her, a strange thing happened. It was a beautiful summer night, hot and still; not a breath of air stirred the leaves upon the trees; and there was no sound. Suddenly the high thorn hedge on their right commenced to rock violently; and behind it there sailed along from the direction of the farm a female figure draped in white. The beholders were spellbound, and they entered the house with bated breaths. There they found that the sick man had just died.

The history of this haunted farm is but another testimony to the truth of the saying that there are more things in heaven and earth than are dreamt of by ordinary mortals. Things such as these are beyond human ken; and in all probability the apparition and the ghost-noises of this old farm house in Godley will baffle the wisdom and the cunning of generations yet unborn.

Author's Note

It is quite probable that the majority of those who read the foregoing account of "The Haunted Farm" will come to the conclusion that it is entirely the outcome of the writer's imagination. I therefore hasten to explain that there is not a single detail in the account which has been imagined by me. Every incident recorded has been supplied to me by persons who have resided in the farm, and all that I have done has been to put them in the form in which they now appear.

Most of my informants are still living; indeed, I saw and interviewed four of them so recently as the last week in March, 1906. One of these was the old lady, who, as a young woman, was one of the lovers mentioned in the account; after her marriage she resided in the farm and is "the farmer's wife" referred to, who witnessed, and stopped the mysterious rocking-chair. The other individuals, who were much younger, related to me the story of the strange noises, invisible footsteps, and uncanny opening and closing of doors, which they witnessed towards the close of the nineteenth century. They are persons of the most reputable character, and of social standing, and they solemnly assure me that the things recorded in the above article are literally true.

I also visited the farm in the month of April, 1906, and obtained from the present occupants their experiences, which are also embodied in the above narrative. The sterility of the "haunted" part of the garden I saw for myself; and can unhesitatingly testify that, from some cause or other, the flowers growing on it are quite withered and weak, whilst similar flowers in other parts of the garden are healthy and blooming. There is no apparent reason for this fact, inasmuch as the unfruitful portion of the ground is as advantageously situated as the rest of the garden.

XXII

The Spectre Hound

ANTIL the latter half of the nineteenth century there might have been numbered among the curious old buildings for which the township of Godley has long been famed, a low, old-world farmstead of the style that is now fast fading away. It was a small, picturesque building, and stood upon a portion of Godley Green, surrounded by a prettily laid-out cottage garden. Its occupants combined farming with other pursuits, and in one part of the building handloom weaving was carried on to a comparatively late period. The farm was pulled down, as already indicated, in the latter half of the nineteenth century; and a handsome modern residence has been erected near the site on which it stood.

There is a curious legend told about this old building. It is said to have been haunted; and the ghost, in the form of a spectre hound, is still supposed to roam at nights over the fields which were formerly attached to the farm. The legend runs that some persons were done to death in some mysterious fashion in the building; and that ever since, an evil spirit, in the shape of a great yellow hound, has haunted the neighbourhood. Old people who can remember the farm, state that in it there was a certain flag on the stone floor, which bore the stains of blood; and that no amount of swilling and scrubbing could ever remove the stains. What became of the stone when the house was pulled down is not known.

Many persons—residents in Godley, and others who have had occasion to be in the neighbourhood said to be haunted—have seen the spectre hound, careering over the fields and through the lanes during the night-time. The occupants of the adjoining farms have been awakened from their sleep in the dead of the night by the noises made by the cattle in the fields; and on looking from their windows have seen the terrified animals dashing wildly across the fields, chased by the horrible form of the great ghost-hound, which

139

with hanging tongue, protruding eyes, and deep sepulchral baying, drove them round and round.

Children, returning along the country lanes from school on winter evenings, have seen the hound dash past, and have reached home well-nigh frightened out of their wits. Young lovers, walking arm in arm along the quiet lanes, seeking some secluded spot wherein to dream of love and happiness, have been put to flight by the spectre; and the more timid maids from the farms have been afraid to venture out after dark.

The wife of one of the farmers, when returning home one night, after delivering the milk in the neighbouring towns, was driving slowly along the lane past the site of the demolished farmstead, when the horse suddenly stood still, and began to tremble violently. At that instant the form of the giant hound, yellow in colour, with horrible staring eyes, sprang from the field, leaped over the fence into the lane, and with great strides like the galloping of a horse raced down the lane in the direction of a well which is sunk close to another farm. Full of fear the good woman reached home, and told her father what she had seen. The old man, merely shook his head, and said quietly:

"The yellow hound. So you have seen the yellow hound?"

"What is it—what does it mean?" asked the daughter.

"Some day I will tell you," said he. "But not now. If you have seen it once, be sure you will see it again."

Some time afterwards the old man himself came quietly home, and told his daughter that he, too, had just seen the hound.

"It was sitting by the edge of the old well," said he, "looking into the water. Its eyes were staring wildly, and foam dropped from its lips."

"What is it—what does it mean?" again asked the daughter.

But the old man only shook his head, and answered:

"Who can tell?"

Again the woman saw the hound in the fields of their own farm, and sometimes it appeared without head. A great hound it was, life-like enough at first appearance, but clearly a spectre, terrible to see.

Another lady saw the hound when she was a child, and

140

several times during her life it has appeared before her. This is her narrative:

"The first time I saw it was in the lanes, when I was walking with a relation, older than myself. I was a child at the time, and although startled was not too frightened to think of trying to scare it away. As it kept pace with us, I looked out for some stones to fling at it; but my relative caught hold of me and said: 'Don't; you mustn't throw at it, or it will attack us, and tear us to bits. It is the ghost-hound.' Since then I have seen it several times. It is not a pleasant thing to meet, and I have no wish to see it again."

Yet a third lady saw the ghost-hound between the years 1890 and 1900. "I was staying at — — Farm," said she; "and I went down to the well to get some water. It was a winter night, and on a pool near the well was a strong sheet of ice. While the buckets were filling I went towards the ice, thinking to enjoy a slide. But when I reached the pool, there stood the hound. It was about the size of a lion, its skin much the same as a lion's in colour, and it had eyes as large as saucers. At first I thought it must have been a lion that had escaped from Belle Vue, or from some menagerie; and as it came towards me I backed away. I was too terrified to turn and run, but kept my face to it, as I retreated. When I neared the house it disappeared. I shall never forget the sight as long as I live. It was a dreadful thing to see."

A tradesman of Hyde—a fishmonger, who made a weekly journey round Broadbottom, and came homewards across Godley Green—once saw the spectre, and his story is equally sensational.

"It was as big as a cow," said he, "its skin a light tan colour. I was walking down the lane with my basket on my shoulder, when suddenly I saw the thing beside me. It kept pace with me as I walked; if I stood still, it stopped, and if I ran, it ran also. I could not overtake it. I was not more than a yard from the hedge, and the ghost was between me and the hedge. I struck at it, but hit nothing; for my hand went clean through it as through air, and my knuckles were scratched by the hedge. My blood ran cold, and I was terribly frightened. Then it ran in front of me, and then came back, and passed me again; it did not turn round to do this, but, strange to say, its head was in front when it returned. As soon as it had passed, I took to my heels as fast as I could run, and it was a long time before I ventured down the lane again at night. When next I met the farmer whose lands were haunted by it, and whom I had formerly served with fish, he asked me where I had been lately; and I then told him I had seen the ghost. He replied that he and his family had seen it often; and that I must not be afraid."

"Never mind about that," I said. "You'll have to do without fish at night, unless you like to fetch it."

"It was the most hideous thing I ever saw. Its feet went pit-a-pat, pit-a-pat, with a horrible clanking noise like chains. I wouldn't meet it again for twenty pounds. I never want to see it again if I live to be a hundred."

And so on, the different mortals who have seen this terrible spectre of the yellow hound relate their grim experiences.

The legend is that the ghost-hound must haunt the lanes and fields about the site of the old farmstead, until the crime for which it is accursed has been atoned for, when its midnight wanderings will cease, and the troubled spirit will find rest.

Author's Note

As in the case of the story of the "Haunted Farm," I desire to state that I have not drawn upon my imagination for any of the incidents related in the account of "The Spectre Hound." The story of the ghost came to my ears from the lips of a friend, and being filled with curiosity at so remarkable a story I determined to investigate it. For this purpose I saw and interviewed all the persons whose experiences are related in the story, and from them I received the substance and detail of the above account. They are all perfectly serious, and positively affirm that they saw with their own eyes the actions of the spectre hound as recorded.

Their statements were given to me in the presence of reliable witnesses; and my informants are still alive at the time of writing (May, 1906).

The fishmonger whose statement is given above is a well-known Hyde worthy, and I interviewed him at his own house on Thursday evening, March 29th, 1906. I took with me two friends—

well-known public men of Hyde—as witnesses. My knock at the door was answered by the fishmonger himself. I told him who I was, and my object in calling—that it was about a ghost, a spectre hound—a great dog.

"Great dog," said he; "why, man, it was as big as a blooming cow. Come inside."

With that we entered the house, and he related the story which is recorded in the foregoing narrative. At the conclusion I suggested that the spectre might have been a cow.

The man shook his head.

"It was no cow," said he solemnly. "It was a ghost. I never want to see the thing again if I live to be a hundred years old."

XXIII

The Boggart of Godley Green

IT would, perhaps, be difficult to find in all England a tract of country of which so many wild stories of ghosts and boggarts are told as the old common land of Godley Green, and the picturesque cloughs and dingles which surround it. Some interesting old farmsteads still stand on and near the "Green," and there were in former times others still more quaint, which have disappeared before the march of time. Concerning most of these homesteads, ghost tales are told; indeed, one old native of Godley recently declared that "there were more boggarts at Godley Green than anywhere else in the kingdom." And perhaps this statement is true.

Most of the stories are old tales, which have been handed down from former generations, no living being laying claim to any personal experience of the boggarts referred to. But in one or two cases the boggarts are said to be still haunting the scenes of their former exploits; and people still living claim to have actually seen the ghosts, as well as heard about them. The present story belongs to the latter class.

There is a certain house in that part of the township of Godley known as the Green, which is said to be haunted by a boggart in the shape of an old lady, who formerly belonged to the house. The legend is not very precise as to the cause of her unrest, but it is said that she did certain things in her lifetime the memories of which will not allow her to rest quietly in her grave. Accordingly, her ghost wanders about the house and grounds, occasionally startling people by its appearance, and its peculiar actions.

One old lady—still alive—gives some graphic details of the boggart. She at one time resided in the house but now she has removed to a distance.

"Many a time," says she, "I have seen 'Old Nanny'—the boggart—wandering about after dark. She is generally outside the house, but occasionally peeps in at the windows. I can remember the old woman during her lifetime, and the boggart is just like her.

144

She wears an old-fashioned cap, and a skirt kilted or tucked up in the old-fashioned style. She wears an apron, which she shakes, and makes a peculiar hissing noise. There is a gate leading from the garden into a meadow and I have seen the boggart standing there, waving her apron, and saying, 'Ish, ish, ish.'"

"On one occasion a relative of the old dame, was present, and saw the boggart. 'It's owd Nanny,' said he, 'reet enough. Why the d— — can't she rest quiet in her grave. What does she want frightening people like that.'"

Another night a serving man was ordered to go into the back garden, and gather a quantity of rhubarb. He was gone a short time, and then he rushed back to the house with blanched face, and terror in his countenance.

"What is the matter?" asked his mistress; "where is the rhubarb?"

"It's where it mun stop, missus, for me," he replied. "I've had enough of rhubarb getting in that garden."

And then he related how he had proceeded to the rhubarb bed, had gathered one stick, and was about to pluck another, when he suddenly became aware of the white figure of an old woman standing before him in the midst of the rhubarb, looking at him intently.

"She waved her apron at me," said he, "and then I heard her say, 'Ish, ish, ish.'"

While he looked the boggart vanished, and then the man took to his heels.

Another lady, who resided at the house in the last years of the nineteenth century, has also some queer tales to tell of the appearance of the boggart. Says she:

"I would not live in that house again if its owner would give it to me, and the land it stands on. The place is uncanny, and the boggart is always there. I saw it more than once. I remember going into the orchard one evening with my sister. We went to pick some apples, and having got as many as we wanted, were returning to the house. At the gate, which leads into the meadow, we saw the boggart—in the form of an old lady, with a withered face. She stood there waving her apron, and saying 'Ish, ish, ish.'"

"We dropped the apples, and fled."

Other persons still alive assert that they have seen this boggart, and it is firmly believed by many that the ghost of the old woman will continue to haunt the house until her sins are expiated, or until some minister or holy man "lays the boggart," by using the forms laid down by law in the olden time, for exorcising evil spirits.

Author's Note

To the two other ghost stories relating to the township of Godley—namely, the stories of "The Haunted Farm" and "The Spectre Hound"—I have thought it necessary to append a note of explanation. I now adopt the same course with regard to the story of "The Boggart of Godley Green." I wish to repeat in this instance that nothing in the story must be credited to the imagination of the writer. All the details have been given to me by persons still living (May, 1906), who have resided in the house at one time or another, and who solemnly assert that they have seen the boggart, under the circumstances related in the above account. Their statements were given to me in the presence of witnesses, and it is impossible to doubt the earnestness and honesty of my informants.

I do not wish to cast any harsh doubt upon their statements, nor do I, on the other hand, desire to give it forth that I am a convert to the belief in ghosts and boggarts. I merely record the stories as told to me by people whose honesty I know to be above suspicion, and who firmly believe that they have seen the things they describe.

The houses and the fields and lanes mentioned in the three stories, as haunts of the ghosts, are all well known to me. I have walked over them alone, at all times of the night and day, and in all seasons. And with the house and grounds mentioned in the story of "The Boggart of Godley Green" I am especially familiar. The land behind the house dips down to a secluded valley; and the gate mentioned by the narrators as a favourite haunt of the ghost is half-way up the slope. It is overshadowed by tall trees, and in certain lights the darkness cast by these trees is peculiar, and almost palpable. Beyond the gate is a meadow, from which at certain times the mists rise thick and white. When seen through the trees the mist sometimes takes strange forms. My first experience of it was rather startling. I had been in the orchard alone one night, and when slowly walking up the rise I chanced to look towards the gate, and there in the gap between the trees appeared a white form, like the veiled and draped figure of a female. It seemed to be moving, and for the moment I received a shock. On proceeding towards the gate, however, I found it was nothing but a moving column of mist, framed by the thick foliage of the trees. Even then, by an abnormal imagination, it might have been taken for a spectre.

But although the mist might in some degree explain away the appearance of "The Boggart" at the gate, I must candidly admit that it does not account for the spectre hound, or the strange noises, movings of furniture, and openings of doors, recorded in the two first stories. These things are as much a mystery as ever.

THE END

www.ingramcontent.com/pod-product-compliance
Lightning Source LLC
Chambersburg PA
CBHW011512170626
46810CB00009B/3337